GRAMERCY PICTURES PRESENTS AN INTERSCOPE COMMUNICATIONS PRODUCTION A DAVID TWOHY FILM VIN DIESEL RADHA MITCHELL

KEITH DAVID "PITCH BLACK" MUSIC BY GRAEME REVELL CREATURES DESIGNED AND SUPERVISED BY PATRICK TATOPOULOS VISUAL EFFECTS SUPERVISOR PETER CHIANG EDITOR RICK S

PRODUCTION DESIGNER GRAHAM "GRACE" WALKER DIRECTOR OF PHOTOGRAPHY DAVID EGGBY A.C.S. EXECUTIVE PRODUCERS TED FIELD SCOTT KROOPF ANTHONY WINLEY PRODUCED BY T

STORY BY JIM & KEN WHEAT SCREENPLAY BY JIM & KEN WHEAT AND DAVID TWOHY DIRECTED BY DAVID TWOHY

PITCH BLACK

www.pitch-black.com

©1999 UNIVERSAL STUDIOS

USA FILMS

D1430291

PITCH BLACK

FRANK LAURIA

Based on the Electrifying Sci–Fi Film

**Written and Directed
by
DAVID TWOHY**

St. Martin's Paperbacks

For Ellen, who's suspicious of dark planets . . .

The darkness drops again; but now I know
That twenty centuries of stony sleep
Were vexed to nightmare by a rocking cradle,
And what rough beast, its hour come round at last,
Slouches towards Bethlehem to be born?

W. B. Yeats
The Second Coming

There are no dreams in cryosleep.

Nothing except the murky sludge of frozen time. Cold and gray, like dirty snow ebbing slowly into a sea of mud. A desolate place where the human soul is hostage, suspended between death and rebirth.

An icy flash of pain speared Fry's brain. She jolted upright, eyes rolling wildly. Dimly she realized she was sprawled on the steel floor, arms and legs thrashing. She struggled to breathe against the leaden weight crushing her chest. Then her skull exploded with sound.

Alarms screamed everywhere, punctuated by the whine of ripping metal and the fiery hiss of white-hot fragments blowing through the boiling madness. All she could see were frenetic strobes of red light bouncing off the white clouds of cryogas choking the cabin. Fry tried to push herself up, but her numbed limbs folded like wet paper. As her nerves blinked awake, they began to writhe in raw agony. The world was dying around her and she was in hell.

An unbearable cold washed over her skin. Fry's mind jump-started, jerking her vision into focus. She was naked, crawling facedown on a sheet of metallic ice. She looked up and saw the floor was tilted at a steep angle, like a sinking ship.

But this ship can't sink, she thought dazedly. Suddenly she remembered.

She'd been in cryosleep, encased in one of four glass locker tubes in the main cabin. Now there was no main cabin. Just a shrieking chaos of shivering pain.

Belly convulsing like a flu victim, Fry groped for the handrail along the wall. When she found it, a faint spurt of energy shot through her arm. Her fingers gripped the frozen metal and she pulled herself erect. Swaying on boneless legs, she held the rail and peered through the hissing steam.

The nearest cryotube was riddled with jagged holes. Fry could see the bloodied corpse of a dead crewie through the fractured window. Lungs heaving, Fry pulled herself along the rail to the next locker. The tube was intact. Inside, struggling to awake, was Captain Merritt. Relief flooded her pounding brain. Instinctively she slapped the intercom.

"Hear me, Cap'n?" she croaked. "Fry reporting. Some kinda compromise to the hull. Holding for now but . . . goddamn I'm glad you're alive . . ."

Merritt didn't seem to hear. He pawed weakly at the glass.

"Gotta pull your E-release!" Fry shouted. "No! Red handle, red handle!"

Slowly, Captain Merritt reached for the release handle.

"I'll get the warmup suits. Wait . . ."

Merritt's mouth opened in soundless surprise as his chest blasted open, spewing blood and steaming organs against the shattered plexi. A quick, hot spatter rained across Fry's naked skin. At the same time she heard the whine of tearing metal as fiery particles drilled through the cabin and detonated a bank of instruments on the opposite wall. A fountain of sparks showered the ceiling and another locker blew open, slamming Fry to the floor. She glanced up in time to see a naked man hurtling toward her.

Fry braced herself, but the collision punched the air from her lungs. As she tried to push the man off, he began squirming frantically. His contorted face floated over her, eyes bulging.

"Why did I fall on you?" he demanded.

Fry shook her head. "He's dead . . . Cap'n's dead. Christ, I was looking right at him. He just came apart."

"I mean . . . I mean . . . chrono shows we're twenty-two weeks out," the man said indignantly. "So gravity isn't supposed to lock in for another nineteen—right? I mean . . . *why did I fall at all?*"

"You hear me?" Fry shouted above the howling alarms. "Captain's dead. Owens, too."

The man seemed perplexed. He blinked sadly, as if about to weep. "Oh no. Not Owens, not . . . oh wait, wait, wait . . ." He grinned at Fry. "*I'm Owens*—right?"

Their eyes met and they gaped at each other like fish in strange waters.

Fry pushed Owens off of her. "Cryosleep," she muttered, struggling to get up. "Swear to God, sloughs out brain cells."

She helped Owens stand then stumbled into the navigation bay. The alarms were louder inside the bay. Skull pounding, she snatched two warmup suits from storage and tossed one to Owens. Still shivering, she fumbled into the plush-lined suit, zipped it up, and plopped down in front of the monitors. She slipped on a headset.

"Fifteen hundred fifty millibars dropping twenty MB per minute," Fry said breathlessly, "*Shit*—we're hemorrhaging air. *Something* got us good."

Owens dropped into the pod beside her. "Just tell me we're still in the shipping lanes," he intoned as if praying. "Just show me those stars, all those bright, beautiful, deep space . . ."

He activated the exterior view. A large yellow planet rushed toward them, almost filling the screen.

"Jesus God!" Fry gasped. "*That's* why we still have gravity." As she watched, the ship's antennae pylons at the side of the screen began to disintegrate in the planet's upper atmosphere. Heart battering at her ribs, Fry lurched out of the pod and staggered along the listing passage to the flight deck, using handholds to steady herself. It was like climbing to a gallows.

"They trained you for this, right, Fry?" Owens called over the headset. "*Right, Fry*? FRY?"

Fry didn't answer. She hurriedly harnessed herself into the flight pod and began running switches. For a moment she couldn't remember, fumbling the sequence. The ship began to roll. Finally she got it right and the ship steadied, its crash shutters sliding back to reveal plasmatic cloud strata sweeping past the windscreen like floor lights in a falling elevator. Suddenly it was as hot as a blast furnace. Fry began sweating inside her suit.

Shedding big altitude, Fry noted grimly. Owens' voice from Nav Bay cut through her thoughts.

". . . crisis program selected Number Two of this system because planet shows at least *some* oxygen and more than 1,500 millibars of pressure at surface level . . . would you *SHUT THE FUCK UP*!"

Abruptly, the alarms went silent. In the sudden quiet Fry realized he must have disconnected the system. She began running a new series of switches. Jettison doors closed around the ship. Fry flipped a security latch and yanked the red PURGE handle.

Instantly a series of bolts exploded in sequence around the ship's skin, blasting away all nonessential hardware that might hinder aerodynamics, including the bulky deep space drives. But as the last section separated the ship went into a dangerous roll.

"What the . . . Was that a purge?" Owens yelled.

"Can't get my fucking nose down . . ." Fry yelled back.

Fry saw the clouds outside spinning like a whirlpool and forced her eyes back to the panel. Fighting back the nausea, Fry threw the actuators and felt the airbrakes deploy. Slowly the ship's roll steadied, but they were still coming in nose high—and much too fast.

Fry pulled an airbrake lever. Stuck. She pounded on it desperately. "*Gonna die, gonna die, gonna die right here . . .*" she chanted, punching the button over and over.

She prepped two more security switches and pulled the PURGE handle. Instantly, two cargo containers blew away from the ship. Fry hoped that by whittling away the extra weight she could correct her glide slope. But she was failing.

What else can I do? she thought wildly. *What? What? What?*

Then she knew. Fry began running more security switches. *All* of them, this time.

Back in Nav Bay, Owens had taken refuge in the familiar parameters of his job.

". . . showing no major water bodies," he droned calmly over the headset. "Maximum terrain 220 meters over mean surface . . . largely cinder and gypsum with some evaporite deposits."

A metallic hiss drew Owens' attention. He glanced back and saw the heavy jettison doors sliding shut behind him—segregating Nav Bay from the passenger compartment. It hit him like a bullet, piercing his belly with cold fear.

"Fry," he called, trying to keep his voice steady. "What are you doing?"

But he knew what she was doing. *The bitch was going to dump the passengers.* She was going to send fifty people crashing to their death on some godforsaken planet. Just to save her own craven ass.

Down on the flight deck Fry flipped another security latch.

"Fry!?" Owens called anxiously. "Answer goddammit!"

"Can't get my nose down," she snapped. "Too much load back there."

"You mean that 'load' of passengers? Is that what you mean, Fry?"

Fry pushed back the savage emotions clawing at her thoughts. There was no denying the math. Either the passengers went or they all died. Fry didn't believe in self sacrifice for some abstract principle. That was for the glory boys playing hero. And she was determined to survive—despite Owens.

"So what, we should both go down, too?" she rasped. "Out of sheer fucking *nobility*? I don't think so."

Thick, tortured silence filled the headset. Trembling despite the warmup suit Fry checked the security latch and stiffly moved her thumb to the button that would jettison the passenger cabin. Spitting out fifty people like some unwanted wad of gum.

Deep inside the darkened passenger cabin someone stirred.

All of the eerily glowing cryolockers had name-plates. The man shaken awake by the ship's erratic motion was called Lawrence Johns. A silver badge beside his name certified he was some sort of law-man. Johns sat up, mind swimming out of the cold, black lake of cryosleep.

Even semiconscious, Johns' thick jaw was set in an aggressive jut, like a truculent bear coming out of hibernation. He ran a hand through his thick red hair then gingerly eased his rigid body to the plexi window.

Johns wiped the condensation mist from the window and peered out at the neon-green rows of cryolockers, glowing in the darkness like unblinking eyes. All of the others were still asleep. Except him. Johns wondered why. He'd always had a cer-tain animal instinct that signaled danger. That instinct had kept him alive across light-years of interstellar manhunting. Then he remembered.

A clammy spasm of fear oozed through his belly as he squinted at the luminous window directly across from his. Riddick lay face up inside the tube, his eyes hidden behind black goggles. The metal bit wedged in his mouth gave him a fixed grimace, like some nightmare clown. The neon readout above his locker said: LOCKOUT PROTOCOL IN EFFECT. ABSOLUTE NO EARLY RELEASE. Riddick's tautly muscled body remained motionless. But Johns knew he was awake. After tracking the vicious serial killer across three galaxies he could *feel* the bastard's thoughts.

Awake or asleep, Riddick was still safely tucked inside the security tube, Johns told himself. The universe was safe—for now. Something hard jostled the ship, and Johns rolled off the cushion. Another blow sent him sprawling to the floor.

Across the corridor, Riddick lifted his head . . .

Fry couldn't bring herself to pull the red handle.

As she bent over the flight panel, fingers poised and hand trembling, Owens' frantic voice crackled in her ears. "Look, Fry, Company says *we're responsible* for every single one of those . . ."

"Company's not here, is it?" Fry shot back. She tried to breathe, but her lungs were fluttering like wings. Her eyes remained focused on the PURGE handle. "I *tried* everything else and I still got no horizon!"

"Well you better *try* everything *twice* cuz no way do we just flush . . ."

"If you know something I don't, get your ass up here and take this chair, Owens."

"When Captain went down you stepped up—

like it or not." Owen reminded, voice tight. "Now they train you for this, so . . ."

"And there wasn't a simulated cockroach alive within fifty clicks of the simulated crash site! *That's* how they train you! On a *fucking simulator!*"

Inside the Nav Bay, Owens unbuckled his harness. *The bitch was about to do it.* "Fry—don't touch that handle!" he shouted, stumbling across the tilted floor.

Fry didn't answer. Overcome by guilt, she stared at the red handle. Slowly, she pulled her hand away.

A huge jolt shook the ship, which began to yaw crazily back and forth, like a pendulum. Fry's fingers went right back to the handle. An electronic readout blinked accusingly at Fry: PURGE ALL? PURGE ALL? PURGE ALL?

"I'm not dying for them . . ." she muttered through clenched teeth. Then she triggered the explosive bolts.

Nothing happened.

Nothing purged from the ship that tumbled through the roiling clouds.

"Owens!" Fry screamed. She knew what he'd done.

Owens had opened the jettison doors locally—and blocked them—defusing the bolts.

"Seventy seconds," Owens announced calmly. "You've got seventy seconds to level this beast out."

Seething with rage and guilt, Fry kicked the air-brake lever. *It broke free*. Two lower airbrakes deployed. The ship began shedding more speed, more heat. Miraculously, the ship started to level off—but the hellish pounding continued. Fighting G's, Fry strained to get a stable view through the windscreen.

The ship had broken through the cloud bottoms. Fry glimpsed a barren landscape an instant before an upper airbrake sheared off and pinwheeled into the windscreen. *The screen fractured into a thousand spider webs*—but somehow it held. Suddenly Fry was blinded by an intense shower of light. Sunlight flared from every crack in the windscreen, flooding the cabin. It was like looking into burning diamonds. Fry averted her eyes and turned to the ground mapping display.

120 meters altitude and dropping like a fiery cannonball . . .

Still inside his cryolocker, Johns heard the rising whine of collision sirens and realized they'd hit a shitstorm. He clawed weakly at the E-release, limbs sluggish and slow. As he heaved himself erect against the crushing G forces buffeting the ship, Johns glimpsed movement through the misted window across from his.

Riddick was rising from his pod like some phosphorescent ghost. The black goggles seemed to zoom in on Johns and hold. And he pulled his lips back in a hideously surreal smile of recognition.

A moment later reality imploded into howling chaos.

Johns was blown out of the cryotube like a champagne cork, coming to rest against the opposite wall. Opening his eyes, he wished he'd stayed inside. Not more than six feet away the hull was peeling open like a tin can.

Johns grabbed a handrail as a blast of wind and sand rushed into the cabin. Horrified he watched an entire bank of lockers tear away and go skittering along the planet floor until it abruptly sank like a stone in quicksand, sucking forty passengers down with it.

The last thing Fry saw before impact was a dark mass rushing at the windscreen.

She braced and shut her eyes as the screen exploded and wind hurricaned through the cabin.

In Nav Bay the chairs ripped from their moorings, slamming Owens against the ceiling. Upside down, Owens saw waves of dirt and debris rush over the floor like roaring floodwaters. Within moments it had almost filled the cabin.

Hammered by wind and sand, Fry opened her eyes experimentally. All she saw was a vortex of motion, of speed, of blurred debris as the ship continued to spin like a drill, burrowing deeper into the alien surface. *Burrowing under*, she thought blankly. Fry pivoted her chair a nanosecond before a black wall of dirt avalanched into the cockpit.

Shock and terror collided in her brain, turning her bones to jelly.

They were being buried alive.

2

Choking yellow dust stuffed every crev-
ice of the ship.

Ghostly shapes floated through the gritty fog,
moaning and coughing, calling out to each other in
a babble of English and Arabic. Johns staggered
past a headless torso, dimly aware of the warm
blood running from his ears. Heart racing, he made
his way to Riddick's locker.

Empty.

Reflexively Johns fingered his holster. It wasn't
there.

No prisoner and no weapon—a terrifying com-
bination. Johns didn't panic. *By the numbers*, he
told himself. The holster must have torn loose in
his locker.

As Johns shuffled across the corridor, a shaft of
blue flame shot through a plexi window. A cutting
torch. Someone was trying to open a jammed
locker. The window fell away and a small, dark

figure crawled out. John realized it was a little girl, no more than ten or twelve years old.

The girl smiled, eyes bright in the dusty gloom. "Something went real wrong, huh?"

Intent on searching for his lost weapon, Johns didn't answer. He didn't see the shape coiled snakelike above him. And he never saw the chained feet lowering silently behind him like a two-headed python.

Johns glimpsed the little girl's eyes rolling upward just before Riddick's ankle chain grabbed his neck and yanked hard, nearly pulling his head off.

Riddick twisted and squeezed, as Johns scratched vainly at the heavy chain. Feverishly, Johns pawed for his baton and flicked it open. As the weighted blackjack sprang out, Johns swung blindly over and over again. The baton smacked Riddick's thighs and groin but the goggled killer clung to a ceiling support and rode out the blows, pulling tighter at the metal noose around Johns' neck. Skull booming, Johns felt himself swimming into blackness. Gathering his strength, Johns grabbed Riddick's ankles and strained forward. One step, then two . . . and suddenly Riddick's grip broke, heaving both men forward. Keeping hold of the chained feet, Johns slammed Riddick headfirst to the floor. He dove on top of the stunned killer and jammed his baton into Riddick's neck.

"One chance and you blew it, Riddick," he said hoarsely. "You never cease to disappoint me."

Johns glanced up and saw the little girl watching him, her face oddly blank.

Fry could hear sounds, but the thick, heavy darkness encased her limbs like cement. Unable to move, she strained to see, but the dust stung her eyes. Abruptly a thin beam of light sliced into the cockpit. As the light swept the cabin, Fry saw it was packed with dirt.

The beam started to recede. "Hey!" Fry called out. "Wait!"

The light curled back. "Hey, who?"

"Hey, me. Over here!"

As the light found her, Fry saw she was buried to the gills. She turned her head and saw a red-haired man bending over her. "Owens?"

"Johns," the man growled. "The name's Johns."

"Carolyn Fry. I'd shake hands, but . . ."

The man managed a smile, then began digging her out. He worked gingerly, as if dreading what he'd find inside the mound of heavy black dirt. For the first time it occurred to Fry she might be injured. As her shoulders and chest emerged Fry pulled her arms free and started to help him. She reached out for the nearest hand hold then pulled her fingers back. It was the PURGE handle.

Johns didn't say a word during the long minutes it took to get her out. He helped her stand, then ran the light up and down her body checking for wounds. Thankfully all she had were a few minor scratches.

"Are there any others, Johns?"

Fry's question failed to elicit a response. Without a word he turned and started walking. Still unsteady, Fry followed.

A sudden blaze of sunlight blinded her and she stumbled forward. Johns took her arm and guided her through the tangle of dirt and twisted metal, to the Nav Bay. Realizing Owens must be inside somewhere, Fry pushed past Johns and began searching frantically, scratching at the dirt like a terrier.

Her fingers found a headset, then a face. Scooping away the loose dirt Fry saw it was Owens, still strapped in his chair. A metal rod shot up from a jagged hole in his chest, like a steel tree with shiny red roots. His blue eyes stared at her sightlessly.

Dead.

Tenderly, Fry reached out and touched his cheek.

Owens' mouth opened. ". . . Out, out, out! GET IT OUTTA ME!"

Fry recoiled and slammed into Johns. At the same time two or three dark shapes loomed up around them. "Ohmigod . . ." someone whispered. "Pull it out of him!" another voice croaked. "Pull it out now!"

Dazedly, Fry reached out.

"No, it's too close to the heart."

"You *gotta* do it, just do it fast . . ."

Fry's fingers brushed the metal rod. Owens swiveled his head.

"Don't touch it!" he rasped, eyes fixed on hers. *"Don't touch that switch!"*

His words shot through her brain, echoing amid the rising jumble around her. Voices and shapes swirled in the dust.

"You'll kill him, I'm tellin' you."

"Shit, just leave him alone."

"Delirious."

"Don't touch that switch!" Owens repeated. Then he began to scream.

"Doncha got some drugs for this poor man?" a voice demanded.

Fry looked up. "All right, all right . . ." She struggled to remember. "Okay, somebody—there's Anestaphine in the med locker at that end of the cabin . . ." Fry half-turned and saw a glaring strip of sunlight where the cabin used to be.

Writhing in agony, Owens' shrieks grew more urgent.

"Get away, everybody!" Fry shouted. She looked at Johns. "Get them out of here."

The shapes melted away, except one. The little girl remained, her features glazed with morbid fascination. Johns appeared and collared her, leaving Fry alone.

Standing in the shadows, his wrists cuffed to a bulkead, Riddick watched Johns intently. His eyes, still hidden by goggles, tracked Johns and the little girl as they moved toward daylight. Then he turned back to Fry.

Still screaming, Owens's eyes were squeezed

shut, so he never saw Fry grab the rod and push it into his heart.

A sudden silence fell over the carnage. Numbly, Fry cradled Owens in her arms.

The other survivors straggled outside, their hair and skin matted with dust.

Zeke and Shazza looked at the forbidding desert terrain, then at each other. They had plied their trade in enough alien wastelands to know they were in deep trouble. All around them was a stark, unforgiving landscape composed of rocks and black sand. The ship had crash-landed in a valley, and the barren floor was relieved only by low hills on one side spiked with sharp earthen spires. Scorching down on everything were two suns—one red, one yellow.

Shazza, the female of the pair, had thick black hair, clear green eyes, and carried herself with a certain savage sexiness befitting a professional space hunter. Zeke, her partner in life, was dark-skinned and powerfully built. His rugged features hinted at aboriginal blood. Zeke and Shazza were registered "bushwhackers," as they were called by the space colonists. Hunters mainly, who took trophies, guided tourists, and occasionally cleared mining areas of hostile beasts. Once in a while they took other assignments for the Company. But nobody actually knew what they did on those assignments. Rumors persisted that the pair were mercenary killers. Whatever they did, they were good at it.

Paris came up to join them. "Well. Our own little slice of heaven," he wheezed, short of breath from the effort. Zeke and Shazza looked at him without interest. Paris was a puff pastry of a man; overfed, overgroomed, and overimpressed with himself.

Behind them, the screams inside the ship rose higher.

"Shouldn't we be looking for the others?" Paris asked nervously, glancing at the others. "Send out a search party or something?"

Johns stared at the desert floor. "I think we found them. Unless maybe some of you boys want to go digging."

The four males standing a few feet away didn't answer. Their head scarves and the religious icons around their necks identified them as Muslims. They were pilgrims on a sacred journey to New Mecca. Three of the pilgrims were young and high-strung. However their leader, Imam, a bearded man in his forties, exuded a quiet, pillar-steady strength.

Abruptly the screaming stopped.

The three young Muslims fell to their knees, as if to pray. There was a flurry of confusion as they tried to orient themselves. Imam separated himself from the group and approached Johns and the others.

"Please," Imam said calmly, "which way to New

Mecca? We must know the direction in order to pray."

Johns squinted at the burning sky and shrugged. He snapped open his wrist compass and checked the readout. The needle was swaying rudderlessly, and the digital display was blank. Zeke and Shazza glanced at each other.

Imam moved back to his pilgrims. He whispered something and they began to rearrange themselves. Shazza saw what he was doing and nudged Zeke who reacted with an admiring grunt.

Imam had devised a way for his pilgrims to pray. Backs together, each man faced a different compass point.

Leaving the ship, Fry passed by Riddick's chained form. *That metal bit in his mouth must hurt like hell*, she thought. *What is he anyway, a cannibal?*

As Fry stepped into the glaring brightness, she saw the survivors gathered on the damaged hull. The pilgrims were circled on the ground, bent in prayer. She moved closer to Johns. "Any others around?"

Johns scowled. "Big talk of a scouting party," he muttered, glancing derisively at Paris. "Until we saw that out there."

Following his eyes Fry spotted the deep, smoldering gash in the ground behind the ship. Whatever was left of the cryolockers was buried in the scorched, smoking grave. There were no other survivors.

"Anyone else having breathing problems?" Paris spoke up. "Aside from me?"

The little girl nodded. "Like I just *ran* or something."

"One lung short," Shazza said, patting the little girl's head. "All of us."

"Well, I tend toward the asthmatic," Paris announced as if the news were of vital interest. "And with all this dust . . ." He looked at Fry expectantly.

Fry was aware that other faces had turned to her. They were looking for answers.

"It's the atmosphere," Fry said slowly, although that part was obvious. "Too much pressure, not enough oxygen. Might take a few days to . . ."

Zeke stepped up. "So what the bloody hell happened, anyways?" he growled.

"Something knocked us off-lane," Fry told him. "Maybe a rogue comet. Maybe we'll never know."

Shazza glared at Zeke. "Well, I for one, am thoroughly fucking grateful!" she said emphatically. "This beast wasn't made to land like this. But cripes"—she gave Fry a quick grin—"*you* rode it down." She turned to the others. "C'mon, you lousy ingrates, only reason we're alive is cuzza her."

The others chimed agreement, moving closer to lay their hands on Fry's shoulders. In the midst of their gratitude, Fry felt a sickening pool of guilt spreading through her belly. At that instant she hated herself.

"Okay," Fry said curtly. "Let's break out the

pressure suits." She led them back inside to the emergency locker. There were a dozen suits hanging from a metal rod. *Like the rod that skewered Owens*, Fry thought. Struggling to erase the image, she began pulling the suits out of the locker and passing them around. "Liquid oxygen canisters are inside," Fry instructed. "Start ripping them out. When you breathe, quick hits only—try to make it last."

The little girl regarded her gravely. "Well, is someone coming for us?" she demanded. "Or are we all gonna die of exposure? Or dehydration, or sunstroke, or maybe even something worse? Hey, you don't have to worry about scaring me."

Shazza gently ushered her away. "We're worried you'll scare *us*," she confided. "Your name's Audrey, right, love? And you're goin' to Taurus Three like us?"

"Yeah, but . . ." Audrey's face took on an impish glint, ". . . do we even have enough food to get there? Or will we have to resort to cannibalism?"

Shazza smiled. "That's quite a vivid imagination you got there, love. Are you travelin' with your mum and dad, then?"

"I ran away," Audrey said proudly. "I'm practically a stowaway. My folks are still back on Scorpio One."

Gutsy little brat, Shazza conceded. *Might make a bushwhacker someday.*

"Cap'n Fry."

Startled to hear her name Fry looked up. Zeke

had a canister in one hand and a knife in the other. "I'll see 'bout makin' this air go a bit further, Cap'n. With your permission a'course."

Fry blinked. *They actually think I'm the captain.* "Go ahead," she told him. Then she found herself staring at another problem. Riddick.

She turned to Johns. "And him?"

"Big Evil? My prisoner—highest priority." He flashed his holobadge.

"We just keep him locked up forever?"

Johns moved to her side. "Be my choice. Already escaped once from the max-slam facility on—"

"I don't need his life story. Is he really that dangerous?"

Johns shrugged. "Only around humans."

Fry glanced at the manacled figure in the bulkhead. He was half-turned so she couldn't see what he was doing at first. Then he shifted his head.

Riddick had his cheek and mouth pressed against the bulkhead wall, virtually licking the metal, despite the bit between his lips. Fry moved closer and saw something shiny sheeting down the wall. Then it hit her. *They were losing water!*

"Oh Christ . . ." Suddenly Fry was running. She snatched up an emergency lamp and started climbing the wall rungs leading to the life-support compartments. Luckily the access hatch was operative. Fry pressed her palm on the ID pad and the hatch slid open. She crawled through the dusty pipes and girders of the superstructure until she reached the water cistern. Behind her someone was clambering up the wall rungs.

Breath heaving from the effort, Fry yanked open a crank-hatch. A bright flare of sunlight illuminated the interior. Numbly, Fry slumped against the wall.

"Well?" Zeke called out, crawling toward her. "Is it just the pump?"

He paused when he saw her face.

"Ask if anyone has anything in cargo," she said woodenly. "Anything to drink."

Riddick could hear Fry organizing the survivors, but his attention was focused somewhere else. Even his pain—his cramped arms, his ripped, bleeding gums—was secondary. His consciousness was consumed with a single imperative.

The abandoned cutting torch lying a few feet away.

With his hands cuffed behind him, around a bulkhead, a few feet might as well have been a light-year, unless . . . Riddick twisted his torso and examined the bulkhead. A section, just above his head, had been fractured in the crash. There was a slim separation in the metal where a chain could slip through. All he had to do was get the cuffs over his head—behind his back.

For a long moment he visualized the task ahead. Then he stood and took another few moments to lean forward and stretch his stiff, aching arms. Suddenly he glimpsed a familiar foot cross the sunlight at the end of the corridor. *Johns*. Fry had left the bounty hunter to stand guard while the others checked cargo. Riddick crouched down and remained motionless, his eyes fixed on the cutting torch.

Riddick knew how to lay low. When he was an elite Company Ranger assigned to Sigma Galaxy, he had learned to remain perfectly still to stay alive. The native life-form on Sigma 3, a large slimy creature his fellow Rangers called Spitfire, had motion sensors instead of eyes. Spitfires lived in the dark tunnels that composed much of Sigma 3's grim terrain. They liked to hunt the humans who invaded their habitat with heavy drills and ravenous greed . . . The human drones so eager to consume Sigma 3's mineral resources and move on—like a pestilence.

At first the Spitfires had it all their way. If one man or thirty were working a tunnel anywhere near a Spitfire's nest, they'd be dead meat. Barbecued meat, Riddick noted without humor. The huge, fanged reptile would spray victims with a particularly nasty acid that seared flesh from bone on contact. The only way to avoid being barbecued alive was to remain totally still, to defeat their motion sensors.

Riddick's rookie job as a Company Ranger was what they called a sweeper. He and two others would clear Spitfires from tunnels that were about to be mined. Their MO was simply to make some noise and scuffle around so as to attract the alien predator. They would throw dice to see who would be the decoy.

While the loser shuffled around the tunnel the other two found shelter and waited. The decoy had to keep his position out in the open until a Spitfire crawled into view, fangs extended to spew its acid venom. Then the decoy remained rock quiet.

If a Spitfire couldn't locate an intruder within a minute its fangs would retract. At that moment it was helpless. The hidden sweepers would "dust" the creature with poison gas that killed it instantly.

More than once Riddick had been badly burned by stray drops of venom.

Then he learned how to cheat at dice.

It didn't take him much longer to learn the Company was running a crooked game everywhere it operated. Riddick was promoted to the prestigious Strikeforce Academy on Sigma 3's moon, where he learned all there was to know about killing. Then the Company turned him loose to enforce security on Sigma 3.

Which was a polite term for slavery. When the murder and torture became too much for Riddick to stomach, he blew the whistle. But instead of reforming the system, Riddick was branded a criminal. The evidence he'd gathered disappeared and he was put in Deep Storage. However, Riddick had been well trained. Before the third year was out, Riddick was out. He overpowered a guard, took his uniform, and slipped free. Once outside he shot two guards and a pilot, and took off with the prison planet's only space freighter. The Company promptly put a million-credit contract on his head.

He became a cosmic outcast pursued by every bounty hunter and bushwhacker in the space lanes. And each assassin Riddick eliminated was added to his list of "serial killings."

Johns had been smarter. He blasted two children to get Riddick's attention, then threatened to execute two more unless Riddick surrendered. There was much Johns would answer for, Riddick mused. And the bastard's time was at hand.

When he felt certain Johns had left, Riddick stood. He moved his shoulders back and forth experimentally. Then he began lifting his arms behind his back, running the chain along the bulkhead. When his wrists were neck-high, Riddick dislocated both his shoulders.

Through the flash of incredible agony Riddick heard a gruesome popping, as his bones tore from their sockets. He wrenched his cuffed wrists above his head, yanked the chain through the narrow fracture, and brought his hands down in front of him.

Calmly, Riddick flexed his body and popped his shoulders back into place.

He was free.

Ignoring the pain shrieking through his arms and chest, Riddick reached for the torch.

3

There was an air of expectancy in the cargo, as the oversized doors rumbled open. Fry, Paris, and Johns stepped into a darkened corridor lined with cargo containers. Leading the way, Fry's light swept past the numbered access doors.

"Mine here." Paris called out gleefully. He pressed a chubby pink palm against the ID pad and the access door rolled up. An interior light blinked on, revealing the contents.

As Johns moved closer, his vision swayed and his legs turned to water. He grabbed a metal rung to steady himself. Fry noticed the lawman's sudden spasm and put an arm out.

"What's the matter?"

Johns pushed away from the rung. "Little swamp flu from the Conga System." He explained with an intrepid grin. "Never shook it with all this cryo-sleep."

Fry saw he was sweating and shivering at the same time. Whatever he had, she hoped it wasn't catching.

"It's all here," Paris cooed ecstatically.

Fry turned and saw why the plump man seemed so happy. The contents of his locker could have stocked a major museum. Tiffany chairs stacked ten high, bronze eagle lecterns, Oriental umbrellas, neo-Egyptian casings, pre-Chrislam chalices—all priceless treasures in the harsh frontiers of deep space.

"King Tut's tomb," Johns muttered, his face set in a greedy scowl.

Paris noticed. "Be surprised what these will fetch in the Taurus system." He crowed. "Here, this Wooten here . . ."

Brushing past the chubby man, Johns lifted one end of the secretary as if weighing it.

"Easy, easy," Paris said breathlessly. "Very rare." He unlocked the top shelf. Cubbyholed inside the small desk were dusty bottles of sherry, vintage port, Cognac, Glenfiddich scotch, Bacardi 151 Rum, and overproof vodka.

Fry was incredulous. "This is it? Booze? *That's* what you have to drink?"

Paris drew himself up. "Two-hundred-year-old single-malt scotch is to 'booze' as foie gras is to duck guts," he informed her haughtily.

"A toast to whatever he said," Johns announced, cracking open a bottle of Glenfiddich.

Paris glared at the burly lawman but he didn't

move to stop him. "I'll need a reciept for that," he said, with all the bravado he could muster. "For all of these."

"Top of my list," Fry assured him. She wondered if Paris was in denial or just totally deluded. Johns passed the bottle and Fry accepted. *No sense wasting 200 years*, she reflected as the scotch burned a soothing tunnel through her tension.

Imam and his pilgrims filed into the cargo area, finished with their prayers. Already a bit tipsy, Fry proffered the bottle. "I don't suppose . . . ?"

The Muslim monk gave her a regretful smile. "Unfortunately, it is not permitted—especially while on hajj . . ."

"Why?" Johns snapped. "There is no water. You understand that, don't you?"

Imam smiled patiently, as if instructing an errant child. "All deserts have water somewhere. It is only to be found. God will lead us there."

For a moment, Fry almost believed him. "Okay, listen up," she said slowly, "we need water, weapons, food, in that order. Go through your lockers and bring whatever supplies you find to Nav Bay. We'll all meet there in exactly sixty tics."

With the muted enthusiasm of children opening birthday presents, the survivors pillaged the cargo lockers, pulling out anything that might qualify as a weapon, or could be useful. Imam found a spare pair of spectacles in his own locker and immediately put them on.

Having accounted for all his weapons, Johns decided to check on his prisoner. But as he moved along the tilted corridor he sensed something was wrong. A clammy film of sweat coated his skin. He hurried his steps then stopped short.

Holding the wall for support, Johns stared at the deserted bulkhead, teetering between disbelief, and grudging admiration.

Impossibly, Riddick had escaped.

Johns hefted his long-barreled laser pistol. *Sure,* he fumed, heading for the bright slash of sunlight ahead. *Like we need another way to die.*

Despite the intense heat outside, Johns' skin still felt cold and clammy. He shivered slightly as he stood on the half-buried hull. Nothing moved on the barren, wreckage-strewn landscape. His eyes swept the area again and saw something glinting on the ground, near the damaged ship. Johns slowly climbed down, pistol ready and senses alert. Riddick liked setting little traps.

Carefully, Johns picked up the shiny metal object. He recognized it immediately.

It was Riddick's mouth bit.

Distracted by the curiosities they'd uncovered, the survivors took the news of Riddick's escape without undue concern. *Because they don't know what he can do,* Johns thought, feeling ill. *He was cuffed behind his back, for chrissakes. Now he's out there—waiting.*

Nobody noticed Johns' distress as the survivors took inventory. Amazingly, for people traveling to alien worlds, there was little food. But Fry had uncovered an ample supply of nutrient tablets. Zeke and Shazza had plenty of survival gear, including a pickax, digging tools, and hunting boomerangs. Johns had a pistol, baton, and shotgun with him, as well as a knife. Imam came up with a ceremonial sword that was more showy than sharp. Along with the liquor supply and delicacies such as caviar, olives, and smoked oysters, Paris had a number of antique weapons. The chubby art dealer struggled into Nav Bay with an armload of curious objects, and gingerly placed them on the floor.

"What the hell are these?" Johns muttered, nudging the brightly painted weapons with his toe. The curved blades looked like long steel fangs.

"Marata crow-bill war picks from Northern India," Paris whispered proudly. "Very rare."

Zeke moved closer and picked up a long, carved wood tube. "An' this here?"

"Blowdart hunting stick from Papua New Guinea. Very, *very* rare," Paris added, with a superior tone. "Since the tribe's extinct."

Zeke snorted and put the tube back, "Extinct cuz they couldn't hunt shit with these things be my guess." He winked at Audrey.

"Well, what's the need for this war party hardware, anyway?" Paris shot back with annoyance. He glowered at Johns like a fat pekinese. "If your prisoner is gone, he's gone. Why should he bother us?"

Johns locked on his eyes. "Maybe to take what we got," he suggested, voice low and tight. "Maybe to work our nerves. Or maybe he'll come back just to skull-fuck us in our sleep."

The intensity in his tone convinced them. Paris' face seemed to pucker up as if sucking a lemon, while the rest began rummaging through the weapons.

The Muslim pilgrims converted to their traditional desert robes, which were well suited for the terrain. Led by Imam, the group also planned to explore the region for water. Fry decided to go with them. However, at the moment, it was too hot to go anywhere. Especially without water. The twin suns blanking out the sky seared through the thin air like cutting torches.

Zeke and Shazza remained inside, working on the breather units. Using tubing and ball-floats, like a snorkeling device, Zeke modified one of the breathers so that it supplied oxygen on demand, rather than a constant flow.

"Here, luv," Shazza beckoned to Audrey. "You give it a try." She helped the little girl strap the unit over her nose and chin.

Audrey sucked on the mouthpiece. A few seconds later she nodded happily. It worked.

"You keep that one, luv," Zeke told her. "I'll make us another."

Fry also kept herself busy during the long hot spell by preparing Owens' body for burial. She wrapped his ravaged corpse, then with Zeke's help put him in the compartment where the other dead crewmen were being stored. By the time Fry had finished it seemed slightly cooler. She went outside where Johns was standing atop the ship, scanning the area with a scope. Sure enough the red sun was dipping low on the horizon. As Fry watched, the yellow sun seemed inclined to follow its mate.

Above her, Johns' scope was trained on a strange blue glow on the horizon. Fixated, Johns watched it slowly spread. *What the hell is that?* he wondered. Earlier he had found sections of Riddick's chains in that same direction.

Fry's emotions were still sodden with guilt. She tried to justify her decision to sacrifice the passengers by reminding herself of the cruel lessons she'd learned as a child. The early death of her space trash parents. The harsh sacrifices she'd endured to get into—and through—the Company's Interstellar Flight Academy. No one had ever cut her any slack. She had to scratch for every inch against treacherous classmates, corrupt officers, and a system designed to eliminate females from command level. And the only way she survived was by being the toughest bitch on the flight deck.

Struggling to suppress her emotions, Fry joined the pilgrims, who were circled in a shady spot near the entrance to the ship. "Imam, we should leave soon," she advised, pointing to the sky. "Before nightfall, but while the air is cool."

The religious leader peered up through his spectacles and nodded.

Zeke's head popped through the torn metal hull. "What? You're goin' off, too, then? Bloody dangerous with that psycho about."

The hunter gave Fry a reassuring smile, but he was worried. *Dishy blond fox like Fry attracts trouble anywhere in space*, Zeke noted. Not that he wouldn't fancy a bit of trouble.

Fry did not return his smile. "We've got to find water," she reminded him brusquely. She gestured at the compartment where the bodies were stored. "Just do me a favor, huh? Get my crewies buried? They were good guys who died bad."

Shazza floated up behind Zeke, her exotic features solemn. "O'course we will . . ."

"Imam!" the pilgrim called Azem shouted, "*Imam* . . . Look!"

Azem was pointing at something behind the ship. Fry rushed to his side, trailed by the others. As her eyes followed the direction of his outstretched arm, her face sagged.

One hundred degrees from where the other suns were setting, *a blue star was flaring into view*.

The dazed survivors gaped at the sun shimmering on the horizon like a brilliant blue sapphire.

"My bloody oath . . ." Shazza muttered.

Audrey stood wide-eyed, her breather forgotten. "Three suns?"

Zeke glanced at Fry. "So much for your nightfall."

"So much for my cocktail hour," Paris said.

Imam remained optimistic. "We take this as a good sign," he declared. "A path—a direction from Allah." He noticed Zeke's incredulous squint and smiled. "Blue sun, blue water."

Zeke shook his head. "Ever wonder why I'm an atheist?"

Johns swung down from the top of the ship and dropped beside them. "I take it as a bad sign. That's Riddick's direction."

Fry folded her arms. "I thought you found his restraints over there, toward sunset."

Johns snorted as if it were obvious. "Which means he went toward sunrise." Reluctantly he unstrapped his pistol and handed it to Zeke. "One shot if you spot him."

"Aw crickey, you, too? *Everybody* asks us that."

Paris wasn't amused. "And if Mr. Riddick happens to spot *us*?"

"There will be no shots," Johns assured.

Zeke's smile faded and he scanned the sunrise horizon, as if the hard blue glare would reveal where Riddick lay in wait.

The Muslim pilgrims chanted from the Koran as they marched toward the rising sapphire star. Johns trailed close behind, providing shotgun escort. Fry brought up the rear, balancing one of Paris' war picks on her shoulder like a scythe.

Fry was already hot and thirsty, and they were just a half-hour from the ship. She wondered if she'd make it back. There was a good chance she'd die out here on this surreal wasteland, under the pitiless gaze of three alien suns. The Muslims didn't seem to care. And at this point neither did she, Fry realized dully. She only wished she had their faith to ease her bleak despair.

"Quiet." Johns whispered abruptly. "*Quiet!*"

The Muslims fell silent. All of them stopped and looked at Johns.

Johns stood still, head cocked as if listening to something.

Suddenly he whirled, shotgun raised. At that moment a string of small rocks rattled slowly down the hillside. Fry glanced at the pilgrims. They all shared the same thought. *Was Riddick stalking them?*

Without a word Johns drifted up the hill to investigate.

Battered nearly senseless by the glaring heat, Fry approached Imam.

"Do you have a cloth I can use to wrap my head?"

The man proffered a traditionally patterned scarf, and helped her drape it correctly, shading her eyes. "Now you are a proper Muslim woman," he said with a reassuring smile.

The headcloth provided instant shelter from the relentless sunlight. Fry took a deep breath through her air tube. For the first time she could look around without squinting. "So quiet," she said, almost to herself. "You get used to the sounds of the ship, then . . ."

Imam blinked at her. "You know who Mohammed was?"

Fry shrugged. "Some prophet guy?"

"Some prophet guy . . ." Imam repeated, as if she had said something profound. "And a city man. But he had to travel to the desert—where there was quiet—to hear the word of Allah."

"You were on a pilgrimage to New Mecca?" Fry asked, trying to be friendly.

The Muslim nodded solemnly. "Once in a lifetime should there be a great hajj—a great pilgrimage. To know Allah better, yes, but to know yourself, as well."

Fry glanced up at Johns, who was doggedly scouring the hillside for tracks. "That's one trip I probably shouldn't take."

Imam smiled and adjusted the scarf securely around her neck. "We are all on the same hajj now."

Above them, Johns swept the area section by section, the way he had been taught at the Company school. No Riddick. But he did spot something else. He took the scope from his belt and lifted it to his eye. Adjusting the lens, the stark shapes outlined against a distant rise came into focus. Like pale green fingers scratching at the desolate rock.

Fry waited for Johns to report, but the lawman remained motionless, intent on something he saw out there. Finally she called up.

"What is it?"

Johns stared through the scope. "Looks like . . . trees . . ."

The news pumped fresh energy into their scouting party. Johns took the lead and the pilgrims chanted with renewed enthusiasm as they trekked across the blistering desert.

"*Allahu Akbar . . .*" they sang as they approached the rise. ". . . *Allahu Akbar . . .* God is great . . ."

Their voices trailed off as the trees loomed into view.

The pilgrims broke into an excited trot, anticipating an oasis. But Fry held back. She took a harder look at the trees. The branches weren't moving in the wind.

Fry glanced aside. Johns and Imam had noticed the same thing.

Up ahead the pilgrims had scrambled over the rise and were now standing silently. When Fry, Johns, and Imam caught up, they saw why.

The "trees" were actually the dorsal bones of a gigantic skeleton, tinted green by lichen. Beyond lay an immense field of bleached animal bones. As Fry stared down at the vast graveyard, she heard a tortured moan, then another. The sounds rose in the wind like tormented pleas from the bowels of hell.

Despite the heat, the sweat froze on her skin, and she began to shiver.

4

Paris had assumed the job of lookout
atop the damaged ship.

As usual, the plump art dealer had seen to his
personal comfort. A veteran space voyager, Paris
knew well the disparity of climate and temperature
one encountered on various planets. He dealt with
the scorching heat by erecting a "misting umbrella," which he had devised for just such an even-
tuality. Normally the umbrella took water, but in
this case sherry proved an excellent alternative.
Paris filled the reservoir with liquor, dialed a solar-
powered regulator, and the umbrella spars shot
cooling bursts of alcohol vapor over his reclining
form.

Paris basked in his electronic oasis like a smug
seal surveying his harem. He turned slightly when
Zeke emerged below.

"Comfy up there?" Zeke inquired gruffly. He
hauled a pickax and coiled cable from the torn hull.

and loaded it onto a crude sled he'd made of scrap metal.

"Amazing how you can do without the essentials of life," Paris gloated. "So long as you have the luxuries."

Scowling, Zeke tossed a roll of tarp onto the sled. He had little use for men like Paris. And he wasn't fooled by the dealer's soft exterior. *Deadly treacherous, like a fat white spider*, Zeke thought. He'd met the type before. If they ran out of food Paris would be first to turn cannibal—if he wasn't already.

Zeke secured the load and glared up at Paris. "Just make sure you keep your bloody fuckin' eyes open," he growled, voice edged with menace. "Don't want that ratbag killer sneakin' up on me bloody fuckin' arse."

Paris responded with an airy wave. But as Zeke began dragging his sled toward the pinnacle hills, the portly dealer lay a war pick across his lap and made sure the razor boomerang was within reach. Then he eased back and poured himself a glass of sherry.

The moment the glass touched his lips, a cool steel blade slid across his throat. Paris went rigid, heart swelling like a taut balloon. Frantically, his fingers felt for the hunting boomerang.

"He'd probably get you right here, right under the jaw," a soft voice speculated. "And you'd never hear him coming. That's how good Riddick is."

Paris managed a deep sigh of relief when he rec-

ognized the voice. It was little orphan Audrey. But
the child had changed her appearance. She had cut
her hair short in the style of her new hero, Riddick,
and found a pair of sun goggles almost like his.

The plump dealer pursed his lips sweetly at Audrey. "Now did you run away from your parents?
Or did they run away from you?"

Audrey shrugged and ran a tiny finger along the
edge of her knife.

The skeletons were huge, with mammoth, hollow
skulls the size of cave dwellings.

Fry and the others shuffled slowly into the vast
boneyard, unnerved by the eerie wailing carried by
the wind. Like discordant echoes of long-lost souls.

"Is this whole planet dead?" Fry muttered.

As if in answer, one of the pilgrims said something in Arabic.

"He asks what could have killed so many great
beasts," Imam explained, voice hushed. They continued farther, pausing before a perfectly preserved
skeleton that seemed part crocodile, part camel—
and all predator.

"Some communal graveyard perhaps, like the el-
ephants of Earth," Imam suggested.

Fry didn't answer. She was preoccupied by one
of the towering bones. She guessed it was a rib of
some sort. But Fry was more interested in the deep
cut marks etched along the bone. Almost as if the
rib had been hacked by a sword.

Graveyard? Or killing field? Fry wondered, inspecting the sharp cuts. She was so engrossed she didn't notice Johns come up behind her. "Long time ago. Whatever happened," he said, as if that solved everything.

Fry glanced up in annoyance. But before she could respond, one of the pilgrims laughed. The sound was oddly out of place. Spurred by curiosity, and a sudden aversion to Johns, Fry hurried to see what was so funny.

It was like moving through an enormous web of hot light and blind shadow. The bones formed a stark, lacelike maze, and Fry circled the edge slowly, rather than lose her way inside. Then a delighted shout cut through the constant moaning. Guided by the sound, Fry ventured deeper and spotted the pilgrims. As she neared Fry heard someone singing.

The youngest of the pilgrims, Rashad, was bent over a giant jawbone lined with serrated teeth. Fist-sized holes honeycombed the jawbone. The constant wind hitting the honeycomb produced the low moaning. Rashad had discovered that by moving his hand over the honeycomb, he could "play" dirgelike music. He grinned at Fry, proud of his new trick.

Well, that answers one question, anyway, Fry thought, glancing around. If Rashad's jawbone resembled a church organ, the skull it belonged to might have been a chapel with a domed ceiling. A very dark chapel.

"Ali!"

Fry flinched, startled by Rashad's cry. She turned and saw Rashad looking for his friend Ali. As Rashad spun slowly in search of Ali, Imam stood unperturbed, as if he'd seen this before.

"Harrh!"

Ali popped out of the darkened skull like a laughing ghost. Then he disappeared again. Rashad started after him, but Imam stopped him with a stern look.

As Imam moved toward the skull, Ali scrambled outside.

"Get out, dammit!" a gruff voice shouted after him. "This ain't no playground."

Fry recognized Johns' voice. Shaking his head at Fry, Imam gave Ali a gentle push toward his fellow pilgrims. Fry knew what he meant. Johns had no right to treat the boy that way—or anybody else for that matter.

"At ease, Johns!" Fry said sharply. "Nobody put you in charge."

"Maybe you better come in here," Johns drawled.

It was more a challenge than a suggestion. Cautiously, Fry moved inside the hollowed skull. Blinded by the darkness after long exposure to brilliant sunlight, Fry stood for a moment until her eyes adjusted. Light streamed inside the skull from various holes, cracks, and sockets, amplifying the chapel-like gloom. She spotted Johns, kneeling on the ground as if praying.

"Look at this," he muttered.

Fry crouched beside him. Johns pointed at a circle of sharp bone chips, illuminated by a slash of light. The chips were about the size of a fingertip. They seemed freshly cut somehow, one side whiter than the other. *Probably those sides were more exposed to sunlight*, Fry speculated.

But Johns had other ideas. "Big Evil is around here somewhere," he muttered. "I can feel it." The lawman hefted his shotgun and stood up. He slowly inspected the inner wall of the huge, hollow skull, probing each shadowy nook and cranny with his weapon.

Despite her instinctive dislike of Johns' crude manner, Fry felt reassured by his vigilance. *Like having a trained pit bull*, she mused. Even though Riddick was probably miles away by now.

The big drawback was, she had to wait there until Johns finished his search. Finally he was satisfied and backed toward the exit. Fry lagged behind, pausing to snap a fresh O_2 unit in her breather.

She was so engrossed in her task that she never noticed the figure dangling just above her head, poised to strike.

It would be so easy, Riddick speculated. He gripped his newly chiseled bone shiv and visualized how he'd do it. First he'd neutralize the woman. Then, when Johns came back to find her he would cut the bastard's throat. Johns would never utter a sound.

But Riddick remained perfectly still, body

wedged in a bony crevice above Fry's head. Intently he watched her step outside. A few moments later he swung down to the ground as quietly as a python. Peering through his goggles he spotted Fry standing just outside the skull, less than an arm's length away. Very carefully, Riddick eased his blade toward Fry's neck.

A shadow crossed the honeycomb of light, moving toward Fry.

Johns took a hit of scotch and extended the bottle to Fry. "Care for a taste?"

She leaned against the skull wall, inches away from Riddick's blade. "Probably makes it worse. Dehydrates you even more."

Riddick's shiv reached out for the back of Fry's neck.

"Probably right," Johns muttered.

Fry took a drink anyway. Just as Riddick's blade extended closer, she stepped away from the opening.

Shit! Riddick fumed, crouching back. *Now I have to listen to their alcoholic bonding.* But he wasn't about to leave until he got what he wanted.

Johns took another swig. "You know, I woulda played road dog for these guys. You could've stayed behind. Probably should've . . . because, you know, if we don't find water . . ." He paused to pass her the bottle. ". . . we may not make it back."

Fry shrugged and took the bottle. "No, I . . . wanted to get away."

"So I noticed. Never seen a captain quite so ready to leave her ship."

Listen to him, Riddick thought, *the slick bastard. She's scared about something and he knows it. He's reeling her in like a hooked catfish.* Riddick eased closer, his bone shiv ready to go to work.

"Better keep moving," Fry said. She handed Johns the bottle and stepped away from the skull.

Johns remained where he was. "What did Owens mean? 'Bout not touching the handle?"

Fry paused and leaned back against the skull.

Son of a bitch, he's got her, Riddick fumed, again edging closer. His anger made him reckless. If either of them had turned around, they would have seen him through the small holes honeycombing the skull.

Johns, too, could tell she was ready, so he pressed. "Hey, see anyone else around here?" He lowered his voice. "Just between you and me. Promise."

When she didn't answer he tossed the bottle aside and leaned close to her. "Carolyn," Johns said, using her name for the first time, "sittin' on our secrets ain't gonna help us now."

Carolyn, Riddick repeated silently. *How can you sit still for this bullshit?*

"I'm not the captain," Fry said slowly. "And during the landing . . . when things were at their worst—Owens was at his best. He's the one who wouldn't let the docking pilot dump the main cabin." She paused to make sure he knew what she was saying. "The passengers."

Johns straightened up. "The docking pilot being . . ."

"Me."

Even Riddick was taken aback by Fry's confession. *No wonder I like her*, he reflected. *The bitch has the makings of a mass murderer.*

This time he would not be denied. Ignoring Johns just inches away on the other side of the skull, Riddick moved—and struck. Deftly, his blade snipped a lock of Fry's blonde hair.

A souvenir of you, babe, Riddick thought, melting back into the shadows. *That's all I want . . . for now.*

"Fuck," Johns said finally. "Guess I'm more glad to be here than I thought."

As Riddick watched them walk away, his goggled eyes looked over at the scotch bottle Johns left behind.

It still had one good swallow.

Johns waited a good five minutes, marching a few paces in front of the group. Then he held up his hand. As the others waited he hopped onto a low ridge and put the scope to his eye. He scanned the boneyard until he found the bottle.

"Didn't bite," he muttered.

"What?"

Johns glanced at Fry and shook his head. Then he returned the scope to his eye and looked again.

The bottle still held that one good swallow.

"Thought he might be coolin' it in the bone-yard," Johns explained. "Could either double-back to the ship or slip in behind us. So I left the bottle out as bait."

Suddenly Fry realized she had underestimated Johns. She also regretted her mawkish confession. *Just deny it*, she told herself. *This is no time to get religion.*

Johns reluctantly came down from his perch. "But nah. Didn't bite," he mumbled, half-surprised.

They resumed their trek in silence. But had Johns taken the trouble to retrace his steps, he would have found the scotch in his decoy bottle had indeed been emptied. *And replaced with sand . . .*

The scouting party descended a narrowing canyon lined with giant rib bones. Fry felt like she was being squeezed inside the belly of the beast. To prevent a panic attack she focused on the sharp pinnacles outlined on the canyon rim. They jutted above them like crooked teeth. *What are they?* Fry wondered. *Mineral deposits of some kind? Or nests for thousand-year-old eggs?*

"Captain! Captain!"

Ali's cry yanked her into action. Fry sprinted to the front of the group. She saw Imam and Johns inspecting something Rashad had found. Everyone was talking at once. *Is it a plant? Looks like a fruit.*

Where did you pick it up? Is it edible? Others were excitedly jabbering in Arabic.

Fry looked closer at the object cradled in Rashad's hands. It had leathery petals that folded back, exposing a hard, stringy core.

"It's a desert plant," Ali declared.

"Maybe it contains water," Imam suggested.

Fry looked closer. "Wait, wait, wait . . ."

Heart pounding, Fry pushed back the "petals" and examined the core. Then she remembered.

"It's a goddamn *baseball*," she said in a hushed tone.

Imam immediately grasped the significance. "We are not alone here, yes?"

They all looked up at the pinnacles that loomed like sentinels above the stark bones, wailing in the wind.

5

Everyone drew a second wind after the find.

Energized and excited, the younger pilgrims led the way, followed by Imam and Fry. Sometimes ahead, sometimes behind the group, Johns roamed freely keeping a wary eye out for Riddick.

Just the kind of thing the smart bastard would set up, Johns speculated darkly, his shotgun tracing an arc as they passed another skeletal hiding place. *Use some familiar object to lure them into a trap. Right up Riddick's alley.*

Fry kept glancing up at the oddly symmetrical pinnacles. Were they mineral deposits, or volcanic cones, or dwellings of some sort? she wondered. Were they connected to these extinct creatures? And what was an old *baseball* doing in this godawful desert graveyard?

"Allahu Akbar!"

Rashad's cry jump-started Fry's heartbeat. She

could hear the note of triumph in his voice. As she hurried after Imam, Fry saw what were emerging from the bone yard. Rashad and Ali were standing on a rise about fifty yards ahead. Johns was trotting up to join them, his shotgun ready.

Too ready, Fry thought. As she headed up the steep rise Fry realized that even the minimal shade offered by the huge bones was a significant relief in the scorching heat.

Sweating profusely, Fry crested the hill in time to see Rashad, Ali, and Johns descending the other side. A small shock numbed her belly.

There at the bottom of the hill was some sort of human outpost.

Fry recognized the type immediately. Aluminex Pre-Fab. Standard Company issue before they discovered that Opalar was lighter, stronger, and cheaper. *Why then wasn't this planet registered?* Fry thought, as she watched the scouting party warily approach the settlement.

"*Assalam ahlaykum!*" Ali shouted.

The trio paused as Ali's greeting echoed through the metallic buildings. Fry and Imam came up behind them. In the silence Fry heard the flapping of tattered window shades. She spotted another familiar shape. A rusty bike lying on the ground.

"*Assalam ahlaykum!*"

"Forget it, raghead," Johns snorted, moving toward the nearest building. "Long gone. Whoever they were."

From the photos left behind on walls and dressers, the settlers had been just ordinary humans. Miners, traders, seekers, all chasing their dreams from tiny Earth into an infinite universe. Although everything was covered with centuries of dust Fry could feel the life in the communal social hall. There were pictures on the wall. Men and women tilling modest gardens. Playing baseball. Posing with children. There was a ping-pong table, and an old holofilm deck.

Fry followed the pilgrims outside. As they moved around the corner of the building, they pulled up short. Before them, in all its rusted splendor, was a moisture-recovery unit. And the ground around it was littered with old jugs.

"Water . . ." Imam said fervently. ". . . water there was here . . ."

"*Allahu Akbar* . . ." the pilgrims chanted.

Imam smiled at Johns. "God is great," he translated. "True, yes?"

"I'm born-again," the lawman muttered, moving on.

Fry veered off on her own and entered another abandoned building. "Lights!" she called.

Nothing. Perhaps the lights were on manual, she reasoned. But after patting around the wall for old-style switches, she came up empty. Through the gloom she perceived a window covered by black-out blinds. She threw them open.

A man was standing right outside.

Fry's breathing resumed when she saw Johns grinning through the window.

"Hey. Don't go too far, huh?" he warned.

Fry nodded. Johns waved and turned away. But just as Fry's heartbeat settled, she heard a loud, metallic creak behind her.

Stiffly, she whirled. Something moved across her vision.

Fry stifled a cry and peered closer. It was an Orrery, a mechanical device that showed the motion of planets around their suns. This Orrery was solar-powered. Slowly it came to life, gears and spokes creaking.

Fry examined the device carefully. It showed five planets circling three suns. One planet seemed always to be in sunlight. *Obviously it's this little desert paradise*, Fry observed. *No wonder the settlers had no need for lights. No darkness.*

She wandered out to the back porch. Ragged clothing still hung from a frayed line strung across the railing. Fry parted the clothing and scanned the area behind the building. *Nothing but hot sand and hard rock, as far as the eye could see.*

Fry started to go back inside, but a metallic glint at the edge of her vision stirred her curiosity. Seconds later she located the source of the glint—and identified it.

Before Fry could move, she needed a few excited hits on her breather. Then she vaulted off the porch and started running.

Fry knew what it was before she reached the grooved runway.

"*Allahu Akbar!*" she shouted breathlessly.

The others appeared and hurried to join her. Chest heaving, Fry just stood there, transfixed by the space skiff perched on the runway like a shiny metal insect.

Digging graves in the desert heat was grueling work. The ground was hard and the twin suns burned down relentlessly, drying the sweat on Zeke's back.

Add low oxygen intake and Zeke found himself gasping before he had completed the long trench that would serve as final destination for the dead crewies. All three lay stretched out beside him, snug in their body wraps.

Zeke glanced back often, keeping the damaged ship in his sight line. He saw Shazza appear beside Paris, and waved. She waved back.

Paris was too busy to wave. Carefully he spooned some caviar onto a toast point and popped it into his mouth. Shazza shook her head in disgust and moved off the hull.

Paris contentedly watched Zeke dig the communal grave. The portly art dealer enjoyed observing physical labor. It *amplified* his sense of entitlement. It was not enough that he was luxuriating, Paris reflected smugly. Everyone else must be laboring.

The misting umbrella threw off clouds of cooling alcohol as he devoured another mound of caviar.

An odd *scribbing* sound stopped Paris in midbite.

Acid fear seeped through his belly and he tasted undigested caviar. Grasping his war-pick, Paris eased out of his chair. He moved carefully to the rear edge of the hull and looked down.

A shadow ducked under him.

"This now qualifies as the worst fun I've ever had," Paris declared, stamping his foot in exasperation. "*Stop it!*"

There was no answer.

Paris slowly climbed down to the ground. War-pick aloft, he checked the perimeter and peered inside the ship. Nobody.

That brat is fucking with me, Paris fumed. Actually he hoped she was. The alternative was chilling. He heard the scribbling sound, and turned.

"Audrey?"

"*What?*"

Confused by the muffled response, Paris moved toward the sound. The voice came from a splintered cargo container, about thirty yards away.

The container was shattered. Blades of sunlight streamed in through the jagged cracks in the hull. Paris carefully stepped inside and found Shazza and Audrey cutting open storage units, looking for useable goods.

"Tell me that was you," Paris said, frowning down at Audrey.

The little girl seemed unconcerned. "Okay, it was me. What did I do now?"

"Assailed my fragile sense of security," Paris intoned. "That's what."

"What're you goin' on about?" Shazza demanded indignantly. The wild-haired mercenary stood up, her green eyes blazing. "That child's been with me for . . ."

They all saw it. The sunlight blinked as someone passed outside the cracked hull. Paris felt a surge of nausea.

"Zeke?" Shazza murmured.

No answer. Audrey sprang silently to the side of the hull and put her eye to a crack there. She saw Zeke in the distance. He tossed his shovel aside and started toward the ship. Then she saw something else.

Audrey whirled back, her lips mouthing a silent alarm. "*Riddick!*"

Heartbeat booming inside his skull, Paris started to tremble. With catlike quickness Shazza snatched the war-pick from his numbed fingers and bounded to the main door. She crouched there, poised to strike. Audrey followed, holding a hunting boomerang. Only Paris couldn't move, eyes bulging from his chubby face as he watched the sun beams blink on and off, one by one, marking Riddick's approach.

Paris felt his legs buckle as the shadow blinked closer.

Suddenly a shape appeared in the doorway and Shazza swung down hard.

"*No!*"

Audrey's cry diverted Shazza's blade. It missed by inches. All three stood frozen, staring at the total stranger in the doorway. Half-naked and half-mad with pain, the man's face and chest were badly burned. His eyes rolled wildly inside his red, blistered face and he stumbled inside, still clutching the emergency release handle of his cryolocker. He lurched toward Shazza trying to embrace her.

"I thought . . . My God, I thought I was the only one who . . ."

Phlup! Phlup! The familiar spitting sound of a magnetic pistol punctured the horrified silence. The man gaped at Shazza in total amazement as he saw bone chips and chunks of brain matter spatter her bosom. Then he realized it was *his brain* decorating her skin.

The stranger sank bonelessly to the floor, revealing Zeke in the background, his pistol leveled. When Zeke saw Shazza's expression he understood what he'd done.

"Oh lord . . ." Paris gurgled, trying not to vomit.

"It was just somebody else," Audrey said in a hushed voice. "From the crash. Just another survivor . . . like us."

Zeke rushed inside. "Cripes galore," he muttered, checking the body. He glanced up at Shazza. "I thought it was him—the murderin' ratbag," he rasped, voice heavy with regret. "I thought it was Riddick . . ."

Not more than twenty yards away—concealed behind a shadowed bulkhead—Riddick watched intently. He knew what it was like to kill someone by mistake. But he really couldn't be sympathetic. After all, he was Zeke's intended victim.

Anyway, he had more important things on his mind. Eyes narrow behind his dark goggles, Riddick stared at the group bent around the dead stranger. *This means he'll have to bury another body*, Riddick calculated.

His gaze focused on something he coveted very much. *As soon as he starts digging, I'll take it*, Riddick promised, gripping his hand-hewn knife.

For a long time, Riddick stood in the darkness, watching Zeke struggle with the stranger's corpse. And as he waited, Riddick's goggled eyes never left the breather unit clamped in Zeke's mouth.

Fry moved carefully inside the abandoned space skiff, checking out the essentials. The working parts seemed to be in order, but time had eroded some of the grav-belts and passenger pods. The cryo system was basic but functional enough to get them to the shipping lanes.

"No juice," Fry reported, testing the energy units. "Looks like it's been laid up for years. But we might be able to adapt . . ."

"Shut up!" Johns snapped.

Angrily, Fry moved to the door and saw Johns facing away from her, his head cocked, as if listening. He turned and shrugged. "Sorry. Thought I heard something."

Fry stepped outside. "Like what?"

"Like my pistola."

For a long moment they both stood listening. Then Johns started trotting back toward the ship. Before he had gone ten feet, Fry went after him . . .

The good news is I left one grave empty, Zeke thought grimly, pulling the sled across the sandy terrain. The stranger's body seemed heavier than usual. Maybe because he was tired. Or maybe because he had killed the wrong man.

Zeke didn't dwell on the question. *Poor bugger would have croaked soon anyhow*, he reminded. Still, it disturbed his professional standards. A man in his business couldn't afford mistakes like that.

When he reached the gravesite, Zeke took three deep hits from his breather before unloading the body. He lifted the sun tarp and hooked it on the sled's rear spar. The tarp provided shade while he filled in the grave. But it also blocked him off from the ship's view.

Wrestling with the stranger's dead weight proved taxing. As soon as Zeke set the body down at the grave's edge he took another long hit from his breather. As he started to roll the body into the grave Zeke noticed something he hadn't seen before. There was some kind of opening at the bottom of the grave. A tunnel.

"Now what the bloody hell . . ."

Zeke hopped into the grave and crouched down at the mouth of the tunnel. There seemed to be some sort of open burrow beyond. Zeke unhooked his handlight and poked it into the burrow.

He never had time to turn it on.

Something hot whipped through the gloom and slashed his leg. As Zeke fell, his pistol blasted a defensive arc. It didn't work. Another slash cut his wrist and the pistol fell from his nerveless fingers.

Zeke clawed and rolled, fighting to escape, but it was too late. Something had him by the ankles. He felt himself being dragged deeper into the burrow . . .

Riddick witnessed most of it. Concealed behind a large pinnacle, he saw Zeke stop, lift the sun tarp, and unload the body. All that time Riddick remained focused on Zeke's breather.

Until Zeke dropped to his knees at the grave's edge.

Riddick's senses began to buzz like bees in a bear's cave. His skull swelled with frantic energy as Zeke suddenly jumped down into the grave. Riddick's trained instincts went into action. Without hesitation he left his hiding place and ran toward the gravesite, dagger ready. He'd been waiting for a chance like this.

Then he heard the magnetic pistol spitting wildly, and stopped short. When the shooting stopped Riddick edged closer.

The grave was empty.

Except for the bloody strands of flesh.

Paris, Audrey, and Shazza also heard the shots. They all looked back, but the sled's sun tarp screened off their view. Immediately, Shazza began sprinting across the hard-packed ground to the gravesite.

Panting breathlessly, Shazza reached the sled and slapped the tarp aside. She froze, face-to-face with Riddick. He was standing on the other side of the grave, his bone shiv raised like a salute.

Shazza glanced down into the grave. And she began to scream . . .

6

Riddick started running the moment she screamed.

He didn't know why he simply didn't kill her, but he had learned to trust his instincts. There was something bad back there—something extremely lethal.

Takes one to know one, Riddick thought mirthlessly, his lungs flailing in the thin atmosphere. Doggedly, he pushed forward, weaving through the dense line of pinnacles. *Thing to do is find cover and regroup*, he told himself. But Riddick knew there was something back there he couldn't handle. *Not alone*.

Blazing pain dropped him to his knees.

Riddick's battle skills understood before his brain comprehended. He rolled as Johns' baton whipped down and slapped the weapon aside. Then he sprang to his feet and snatched at Johns' shotgun. Unfortunately he missed. Johns didn't.

The lawman clawed at Riddick's goggles and connected. The moment Johns pulled them off, Riddick was helpless. The blaring sunlight exploded against his exposed vision like a nuclear blast. Shiv blindly slashing empty air, Riddick fell back.

Johns pounced like an enraged beast. Unable to see, Riddick tried to shield himself against the blows whacking his unprotected body. But it wasn't enough. Johns swung down hard over and over, smacking ankles, knees, back, kidney . . . anywhere Riddick rolled, Johns was there.

"Want me to X your vampire ass? That it?" Johns grunted, baton rising and falling like an axe. "Cuz you are *testing me*, Riddick! Same crap— different planet. As God is my secret judge, you are sorely testing my righteous good nature."

Agony ripped through Riddick's flesh and his brain began to spin with nauseating speed. Suddenly more hands were beating him, pushing him toward the sickening blackness. He tried to see but when he opened his eyes blinding pain seared through his skull like a laser. Through the shrieking confusion he heard the woman's voice.

"What'd you do with him? You bloody sick animal! What'dja do with me Zeke?"

"C'mon, Riddick," Johns rasped, his pounding baton punctuating his words. "Tell us a better lie!"

"Ease up! Ease up! Shazza!"

Dimly Riddick recognized Fry's voice.

"Just tell me . . . *what*?" Fry demanded. "What's going on?"

"Don't you here them *sounds*?" Riddick groaned. "*Listen!*"

"Just kill 'im," Shazza shouted breathlessly, kicking and hitting Riddick's curled body. "Just somebody kill 'im before he can . . ."

Hands pulled Shazza back, but she landed one last kick to Riddick's face. Blessedly, the pulsing agony dissolved into a deep, dreamless vortex.

Shazza stared down at the bottom of the grave Zeke had dug.

Twenty years, she thought ruefully. *Twenty fantastic years of incredible excitement, wonder, discovery, and yes, wild romance. Twenty years of absolute trust, and unconditional friendship. Twenty years of chasing violent death and fabulous treasure on alien worlds. And it all comes down to this. A few bloody fucking entrails at the bottom of an open grave.* The gruesome little pile of ragged meat was all that remained of her Zeke, her love, her life . . .

Shazza looked up and saw Fry and Johns approaching. She didn't want to talk to them. She didn't want to talk to anybody. All she wanted was a chance to fillet Riddick alive, slice by agonizing slice.

Fry watched Shazza stalk away with a mixture of sympathy and apprehension. In her present emotional state, Shazza could snap at any second. Which could get them all killed.

But looking down at the blood-caked strings of

human flesh, Fry understood Shazza completely. *What kind of degenerate would do something so vicious?* Fry reflected. But something else nagged at her thoughts.

It hardly seemed possible that Riddick could have killed Zeke, hack him to pieces, and get rid of the body so quickly. She glanced at Johns. The lawman had Riddick's confiscated bone shiv in his hand. The crude weapon shone gleaming white in the glare.

"He used that?" Fry asked.

Johns lifted the weapon, turning it in the harsh light. "Sir shiv-a-lot. He likes to cut."

"So why isn't it all bloody?"

Fry's question drew an annoyed scowl. "I assume he licked it clean," Johns said, voice heavy with contempt.

Fry wasn't convinced. Riddick's clothes were also blood-free. There was no way he could have washed them clean, even if there was any water on this desolate rock. *And what did he do with Zeke?*

Ignoring Johns, she turned and walked back to the ship, brain crowded with doubts.

The cracked interior of the ship offered relief from the relentless glare. She stood in the shadows for a few moments, gathering herself. Then she moved farther back into the cargo container where Johns had secured his prisoner.

Bound in chains, Riddick sat on his haunches in the darkest corner of the bulkhead, eyes closed tight, and head down. What Fry could see of his body was a mass of bruises, and there was a nasty swelling at his temple.

"So where is he?" Fry asked quietly.

Riddick didn't stir.

"Tell me about the sounds," she persisted. "You said you heard something . . ."

He didn't move a muscle. He could have been made of stone.

"If you don't talk to me, Shazza'll take another crack at it—at your skull."

"You mean the whispers?" Riddick's voice had a taunting edge.

"What whispers?"

"The ones tellin' me to go for the sweet spot . . ." he said, voice soft and dreamy. "Just left of the spine, fourth lumbar down. The abdominal aorta. Oh yeah. What a gusher. Had a cup on his belt. So I used it to catch a little spill. Metallic taste to it, human blood. Copperish. But if you cut it with peppermint schnapps that goes away." He added slyly, "Course that's more for winter. Summertime I like mine neat."

Fry stared at the crouched, battered figure. *The son of a bitch is pulling my chain*, she decided. Riddick seemed to relish playing the role of resident boogeyman.

"Why not shock me with the truth now?" Fry asked calmly.

Riddick shook his head in disgust. "All you people are so scared of me . . . and most days I'd take that as high praise ... *but it ain't me you gotta worry about now*."

If he was trying to scare her, it worked. Fry tried to bury the fear with anger.

"Show me your eyes," she ordered. "*Show me*, Riddick!"

There was something both mocking and sensual in the way Riddick slowly raised his head and opened his eyes. His eyelids fluttered as if sensitive to even the faintest light. Then, almost shyly, they lifted.

An awed shiver split Fry's belly. His eyes gleamed like luminous black pearls. Imbedded deep within the huge, shiny pupils were tiny yellow jewels that burned as bright as the twin suns outside. Riddick's black-sheened gaze was profoundly unsettling. Like the flat, pitiless stare of a starved jaguar.

"Wow ..."

The familiar voice shattered the moment.

Fry whirled and saw Audrey lurking in the shadows. The little girl's mouth sagged in rapt admiration. "How can I get eyes like that?" she asked fervently.

Fry pointed at the door. "Out!"

"Well first you gotta kill a few people," Riddick said, ignoring Fry.

Audrey did the same. "Okay. What else?"

"Not okay." Fry snapped. "*Leave*, Audrey."

Riddick continued as if he hadn't heard. "Then you gotta get sent to some slam where they tell you

you'll never see daylight, never again. So you dig up a doctor . . . one that ain't totally stoned and de-boned . . . and you pay him 2C menthol Cools to do a surgical shine job on your eyeballs."

"So you can see who's sneaking up on you in the dark," Audrey whispered.

"And cut his ass down first," Riddick finished emphatically.

Fry swooped down on Audrey and physically ejected her.

"Cute girl," Riddick observed.

Fry's voice had a threatening edge. "Let's keep her that way."

Riddick settled back, liquid eyes regarding her calmly. "Well, so maybe I did X out a few lives," he admitted. "But not this one. No, ma'am, not Zeke-man. You got the wrong killer."

"Then where is he?" Fry demanded. "He's not in the hole. We looked."

"Look deeper," Riddick told her.

Then he closed his eyes and smiled. As she stood watching, he began to make *clicking* sounds with his tongue.

Like the clip-clopping of hoofbeats, Fry noted vaguely. But she didn't know what it meant.

The scouting party wasn't going too far.

Fry led the way, a chain looped over her shoulder. Audrey and Shazza were right behind her, closely followed by Imam. Johns trailed them reluctantly as they marched out to the gravesite, complaining all the way.

"I *know* what happened," he grumbled. "He went off on the guy, buried him on the hill somewhere, and now he's trying to . . ."

"Let's just be sure," Fry said over her shoulder.

"I *am* sure. Look, murders aside, Riddick belongs in the Asshole Hall of Fame. He loves that jaw-jackin', loves makin' you afraid, cuz that's all he has. And you're playin' right into . . ."

"We're gonna find the body, Johns," Fry shouted. "Christ, you're a cop. Why do I have to tell you this? We gotta go down and find it."

"Hey, if you're afraid, I'll go," Audrey offered.

Fry wasn't amused. "Nobody has to go down there but me, okay?"

Johns caught up and pulled Fry aside. "Look, being ballsy with your life now doesn't change what came before . . . It's just stupid."

His words hit a nerve.

Fry jerked her arm free. "What, you think I'm doing this to prove something?"

"Well?" he sighed. "Are you?"

Fry didn't answer, She turned and headed toward Zeke's grave, wavering between raw guilt and righteous indignation.

Spurred by Johns' accusation, Fry didn't pause to think. As soon as they reached the site, Fry hooked one end of the long chain to her web belt, handed the chain to Shazza, then dropped into the deep grave.

Letting her eyes adjust to shadow, Fry circled Zeke's tattered remains and spotted his handlight. She picked it up. Broken. Then she saw it.

There was a narrow burrow at one end of the grave. Fry looked up. The ridge of pinnacles began a few yards away. Maybe the burrow connected to the pinnacles, Fry speculated. Or maybe it concealed Zeke's body.

She decided to find out. Letting the safety chain play out behind her, Fry entered the cramped tunnel. A few feet above, Shazza, Audrey, and Imam let the chain slide through their hands as she crawled out of sight.

The tunnel went deeper underground then took an uphill turn. It also became narrower. Fry glimpsed a spray of light ahead and wormed forward.

She didn't like tight places. It occurred to Fry that she might not be able to exit as easily as she entered. Still, she inched toward the light.

Fry's tenacity was rewarded. The tunnel opened into a cool chamber, large enough to stand. She saw bones scattered about the hard ground. A shaft of light illuminated the center of the round floor.

Fry looked up. It was an earthen funnel—the center of a pinnacle.

They're hollow, she thought with a measure of surprise. Like silos.

CLICK. . . . CLICK . . .

The sound froze her heartbeat.

CLICK . . . CLICK . . . CLICK . . .

Slowly, Fry turned toward the sound. *There's something here*, she realized.

Something rustled just beyond the cusp of light from the funnel. Something *unfolding* . . . Fry's blood turned to ice. Soundlessly she began back-tracking along her chain.

But as she turned, *a shadow moved across the exit.*

It stopped her dead. She crouched down, and her hand brushed something moist. She picked it up and angled it toward the light. It was Zeke's boot.

And part of Zeke was still in it.

CLICKETY-CLICK . . . CLICKETY-CLICK . . .

As the sound rose the entire chamber came alive around her. Shadows unfurled like looming squid, skulking around the perimeter of light, circling . . .

A lightning-fast strike speared Zeke's boot right out of her hand!

Fry made her move. She rolled back into the shaft of light and jumped. Her fingers found pur-chase on the side of the pinnacle, and her toe caught a rock spur. Driven by naked terror Fry braced her back against one wall, her feet against the other, and started inching up to the open light.

Halfway up, her safety chain went tight. Fry pulled, but the chain wouldn't budge. *Is it caught on something?* Fry wondered. *Or did something catch it? Like Zeke's boot.*

Either way it was cause for panic. Fry started pounding the earthen wall.

"Here!" she shouted. "I'm in HERE! *HERE!*"

CLICKETY-CLICK, came the answer.

Suddenly her panic disintegrated into raw terror. *Something tugged at her chain from below.*

Wildly, Fry kicked and clawed at the earthen walls, trying to gouge out footholds.

"I'M OVER HERE . . . IN HERE . . ." she cried. Then her voice turned to stone.

The weight on her chain was stronger now, pulling her down. Fry's hold began slipping, dragging her closer to the madly clicking lair below. Frantically she tried to jettison her belt but couldn't brace herself. Her feet scrambled like a rat in a treadmill as the chain drew her back to the rustling horror.

7

Audrey felt Fry's safety chain tighten. At the same moment a faint echo drifted up from the grave.

"Did you hear . . . ?" she hissed, falling to her knees. The others dropped down beside her, their heads suspended over the grave. They heard nothing.

Then the chain began to snake through their hands . . .

Fry managed to find a precarious hold, halfway up the funnel. But the chain kept her from making it to the open air. Her breath came in shivering gulps and her muscles were cramping in the stifling space. She looked up at the blank patch of sky, trying to blot out the gibbering terror below. But all she saw were Zeke's ravaged entrails. The chain pulled harder, as if more hands were at work, and she began to slide.

Desperately her fingers raked the earthen wall, but she kept sliding down. Inch by frantic inch she was being dragged into hell.

Something exploded near her head! Fry screamed as the wall crumbled and dark figures loomed over her. Vision blurred by the sudden daylight, Fry made out faces. *Human faces.*

She recognized Shazza as she broke through the wall with a pickax, and saw Imam reach inside for her. Johns appeared beside him, and the two men hauled Fry into the open air.

"We got you . . ." Johns huffed as he pulled her up. "It's okay . . . it's okay. We got you now."

Fry realized she was still yelling. She closed her eyes. When she opened them again, she saw Imam's concerned expression. He peered at her through his spectacles.

"The child heard you before any of us could even—"

Shazza cut in front of Imam. "Did you find him?" she pleaded, face ragged with grief. "You find Zeke?"

Fry's brain reeled at the memory. ". . . Wasn't Riddick," she panted, ". . . it was . . . it was . . ." She grabbed Shazza's mouthpiece and took a long hit of oxygen. "Goddamn that was stupid . . . but wasn't Riddick," she rambled breathlessly. "Something else down there that got Zeke and nearly got—"

Without warning she tumbled back inside the

pinnacle. *Something still had the chain. Something very strong.*

The others grabbed her flailing limbs, preventing her fall. It became an eerie tug of war between the human hands above and the unseen alien "hands" below. And the humans were losing.

First Audrey lost her grip, then Fry's ankle slipped out of Shazza's sweaty palms. Only Johns and Imam kept her from falling completely through. Then Imam let go. Too frightened to scream Fry braced for the final drop.

Suddenly the chain dragging Fry down broke away. She opened her eyes and saw Imam bending over her with a knife. He had cut through her belt.

Sobbing hysterically, Fry crawled to the safety of flat, hard ground.

The survivors were on a mission. They went about their business with military precision, packing O_2 units, liquor, umbrellas, weapons, canned delicacies, the Koran—whatever qualified as essential.

Imam helped Fry pull a power cell from the ship's battery bay. The cell's lead exterior made it extremely heavy. They managed to slide it out but weren't strong enough to keep the unit from hitting the metal deck. The fall put a dent in the soft lead lining. Fry prayed it wasn't damaged.

"One is all?" Imam asked.

She glanced at the heavily loaded sled outside. "For now."

As Audrey helped Paris carry a small chest of

food and whiskey, she paused. Paris started to speak, then changed his mind when he saw the rapt concentration on the little girl's face. *She was listening to something.*

Audrey lifted her goggles and turned toward the pinnacle hills as the strange whispering echoes drifted in the wind . . .

Johns went to his locker to take care of his firepower. He dug out a box of blue-metal shotgun shells and put them aside, rummaging in his drawer until he found a red shell. The red boy was his own special blast, Johns reflected. With great care he tucked the red shell into a secure pocket.

As he left the locker he racked the blue shells into his shotgun and cocked the power grid. Then he ambled over to Riddick's quarters.

The prisoner was where Johns had left him, chained in a dark corner of the bulkhead. Riddick was crouched down, eyes shut, but he seemed to feel Johns' shadow fall over him. Slowly he lifted his head and smiled.

"Found somethin' worse than me, huh?"

"We're movin'." Johns hefted his weapon. "And I'm just wonderin' if I shouldn't lighten the load right now."

Riddick got to his feet. His eyes opened slightly and fixed on Johns.

Johns pointed the shotgun at Riddick's head.

"Woof, woof," Riddick said softly.

Johns pulled the trigger.

The flat magnetic pulse exploded in the cramped

space. Ion fumes hung in the stale air as Johns
peered at Riddick's fallen body. A moment later
Riddick stirred.

Johns watched him get to his feet. The shotgun
had discharged past his head and shattered his wrist
chains. "Want you to remember this moment, Riddick," Johns said. He pointed his weapon at the
smoking gash in the metal wall. "The way it coulda
gone—and didn't."

Riddick fingered his ear. "Say that again? Blast
made me slightly deaf."

"Here's the deal," Johns snapped, bringing the
weapon back. "You work without the chains, without the bit—without the shivs. You help us get off
this rock . . ."

"For what?" Riddick snorted. "The honor of
goin' back to some asshole of a cell?"

Johns lowered the shotgun. "Truth is, Riddick,
I'm tired of bumpin' titties all the time. I wanna
be rid of you as much as you want to be rid of
me."

In the brief silence Riddick calculated the possibilities. The future rearranged itself like cherries
on a slot machine.

He regarded Johns with a sly, narrow-eyed
smile. "You'd cut me loose, boss?"

Johns reached out and offered him the spectrum
goggles to seal the deal. "Only if we get out of this
alive. And there may be a way."

Riddick stared at the goggles in Johns's hand.

"My recommendation," he said quietly, "do me. Don't take the chance I won't get shiv-happy on your wannabe ass." He looked up, eyes gleaming slits. "Ghost me, Johns. Would if I were you."

Johns kept his hand out. "If you were me, I'd kill us both. C'mon, you wanna sit at the grown-up table or not?"

Hesitantly Riddick reached out for the goggles.

In a blurred instant he snatched the shotgun with his other hand—and suddenly Johns was staring into the blank eyes of his own weapon.

"Want *you* to remember this moment," Riddick mocked. He pumped the shotgun, spitting blue shells over Johns' chest. Then he took the goggles and walked away, tossing the empty weapon aside as he headed for daylight.

The blue sun was lowering, casting purple and indigo shadows across the harsh landscape. Far ahead, the edge of the desert seemed to be on fire, as the yellow and red suns rose above the horizon. The merging light turned the sky green, amplifying the nightmarish urgency of their exodus.

The pilgrims marched stolidly, no longer singing. Fry and Imam had fixed up a sling for the power cell and were carrying it like a baby in a hammock. Behind them Riddick was dragging Zeke's heavily loaded sled.

From pycho-beast, to beast of burden, Riddick noted ruefully. He'd traded his wrist chains for shoulder chains. But now that he could see again, anything might happen.

Huffing from the unfamiliar exertion, Paris left Shazza and little Audrey to carry the food chest while he hurried to catch up to Johns. "So just like that," he whined. "Wave your little wand and he's one of us now."

Johns shrugged. "Didn't say that. But this way I don't have to worry about fallin' asleep and not wakin' up."

"Well, I feel we owe Mr. Riddick amends," Imam reminded.

Shazza stiffened. "Oh right. Let's all line up and beg his forgiveness. Right you are." But as she strode ahead, dragging Audrey along, Shazza felt a pang of guilt.

"At least give the man some oxygen," Imam said.

They all glanced back at the goggled figure towing the heavy sled in the relentless heat.

"He's happy just bein' vertical," Johns said curtly. "Leave him be."

"So I can talk to him now?" Audrey inquired sweetly.

"*No!*" Johns, Shazza, Fry and Imam said in unison.

Feeling weak, Paris dropped one of his wine bottles. Trailing just behind, Riddick scooped it up. Paris stopped and held out his hand.

"Paris P. Ogilvie. Antiquities dealer, entrepreneur."

Riddick solemnly shook his hand. "Richard B. Riddick. Escaped convict, murderer." He lifted the wine bottle, cracked the neck against the sled, and took a long satisfied swallow.

Heart pumping, Paris scurried ahead to join the others. "You know," he declared loudly. "If I owned hell, and this planet . . . I believe I'd rent out this planet and live in hell!"

No one answered. They were all staring at the row of pinnacles high above them.

Fry shivered. Then she heard it.

CLICKETY-CLICK.

The sound pierced her belly like an icy spear. Fear flooded her limbs and she stopped. The others did the same.

CLICKETY-CLICK.

Fry's neck hairs rose. Within seconds, the sound had faded.

The group started moving again, a little faster.

CLICKETY-CLICKETY-CLICK.

Were they being stalked? Fry wondered anxiously. Trying to stay calm, Fry moved backward trying to trace the direction of the sound.

Then she spotted them.

The sound was coming from the prayer beads dangling from Rashad's belt. Whenever the young pilgrim moved, the strings *clacked* together.

Fry's sense of relief evaporated when they reached the space skiff. The craft seemed much older than she remembered. As if it had flown a few war missions in their absence. But at the moment the battered skiff didn't look as if it would ever fly again.

Paris examined the craft and shook his head. "I mean . . . usually I can appreciate antiques, but, uh, *this* . . ."

Johns was more direct. "Little ratty-ass."

Fry struggled to get the power cell aboard the skiff. "Nothing we can't repair," she assured. "So long as the electrical adapts." But she was still worried about the dented cell.

"Not a star-jumper," Shazza observed.

"Doesn't need to be," Riddick told her. "Use this to get back up to the Sol Track shipping lanes. Stick out a thumb. You'll get picked up." He turned to Fry. "Right?"

Fry glanced from Riddick to Johns. *How does he know that?* she wondered. Fry turned her attention to the leaden power cell. "Little help here?"

Imam and Fry muscled the cell onto the ship, but they were finding it difficult. Riddick moved to lend a hand but Johns blocked the door. He didn't want Riddick inside the ship. The bastard might get funny ideas.

"Check those containers over there," Johns suggested. "See what we got to patch wings with."

Riddick didn't argue. His time would come real soon now.

The young pilgrims took it upon themselves to repair the moisture recovery unit. They attacked the project with religious fervor, knowing Allah had led them to the task. And in a universe of infinite possibilities, they were mathematically correct. It was, after all, a totally random collision of faith and necessity.

A hundred yards away, God was a minor part of the equation as Imam helped Fry adapt the power cell to the skiff's outdated electrical system. Fry locked the cell in place and reached for the ON handle. Without so much as a prayer she pulled it down.

A long minute later the console flickered and went dark. Then the ship's interior lit up in sequence, like a holiday billboard.

"Praise Allah," Imam intoned. But he was premature.

"Okay, this should buy us a Sys-Check," Fry reported. "But we'll need more cells."

"How many?" Johns asked.

"Fifteen six-gigs here . . ." Fry calculated. "Ninety gigs total . . . other ship carries twenty-gig cells, so . . . five. Five total to launch."

"Fifty kilos each, huh?"

It wasn't a question. Fry knew as well as Johns did it would take them another grueling day's march to transport the cells.

"Old Sand Cat outside," Shazza offered. "See if I can't get it up and chuggin'."

Fry grinned, bolstered by Shazza's suggestion. The Sand Cat would make the whole thing doable. The vehicle was designed to haul mining samples

over alien terrain and had proven to be an inter-
galactic workhorse.

"Do it," Johns said emphatically. "And if you
need an extra hand, just tap our problem child out
there." But as Johns glanced out the window, his
air of certainty disintegrated.

"Where's Riddick?" Johns rasped, voice tight.

Nobody answered . . .

Riddick was walking the ghost town. He found
dead gardens . . . upended chairs and furniture . . .
broken skylights . . . scattered utensils. *All signs of
an untimely bug-out*, he speculated, examining a
spoon through his dark goggles.

A few yards away Audrey and the young pilgrim, Ali, stood watching him. Audrey was wear-
ing her makeshift goggles in homage to her hero,
and Ali had shaved his head. Both waited for their
outlaw guru to uncover some alien secret.

But Riddick remained mystified by what he
found. He approached the entrance to a tall, win-
dowless structure. The metal door was crusted with
rust and dirt. Locked. Moving around the side of
the building Riddick found a small, filthy window.
He rubbed away some dirt and peered inside. *A
shadow seemed to shrink across the wall.*

Riddick lifted his goggles and took another look.
His watery pupils saw broad details of the interior;
shelves, crates, and a tall, metallic shaft in the center of the dark room. Everything was still.

Covering his eyes, Riddick moved back to the

entrance. He had only taken a few steps when he noticed a metallic glint on the ground. He crouched down and raked the dirt with his fingers. He excavated a pair of broken eyeglasses, a shattered handlight, and a child's toy robot.

Watching from a short distance away, Audrey and Ali exchanged excited glances. Their leader had discovered something.

Riddick rubbed the robot's solar panel clean. The toy's language program warbled to life. ". . . to all intruders. I am the guardian of this land. I will protect my masters at all cost. Death to all intruders."

As Riddick stood up he saw a narrow door that was obscured by years of windblown dust. He moved closer. The door was chained. There was a panel beside the door. Riddick brushed away the caked dirt. It was a sign that read CORING ROOM.

A familiar rasp cut through the quiet. "You're missin' the party, c'mon."

Riddick didn't bother to look. He knew it was Johns, keeping him on a short leash. He backed away from the door and turned. Johns was stationed a few yards away, his shotgun at high port. The lawman grinned.

Suddenly, Riddick whirled and kicked out hard against the door. "Missin' the party, c'mon," he mimicked.

A dim chorus of cheering voices floated up from the main building.

Ignoring Johns, Riddick marched back in the di-

rection of the cheers. Johns fell into step behind
him, shotgun on his shoulder.

Audrey crawled out of her hiding place. She had
taken refuge in a trash bin when Johns appeared.
"Missin' the party, c'mon," she called out to Ali.

Receiving no answer, Audrey adjusted her goggles and started after Riddick.

Ali watched her go, with mixed feelings. He
liked his new friend, but she was after all, a girl.
Exploring alien worlds was man's work, Ali
thought loftily as he approached the door Riddick
had struck. Still locked tight. Ali moved around
and peered through the small window. The metal
door was chained shut from the inside.

But Riddick's kick had bent the door, making a
small opening, barely large enough for Ali to
squeeze through. Wait until the others heard about
his adventure, Ali gloated, crawling inside the dark,
deserted room. Maybe then they'd start treating
him like a man, instead of a boy.

By the light trickling from the window, Ali began to explore. He knew enough about mining
techniques to recognize the coring drill in the mid-
dle of the room. He moved closer. The drill's di-
amond bit was somewhere at the bottom of the dark
shaft. Ali wondered what they were mining for. He
moved back to the window and saw a flat metal
disc on the sill. Ali brushed the dust off the disc.

It was a solar panel. The moment Ali exposed it
to light, the disc began to revolve, orienting itself
to the sun. Mouth open, Ali watched with a mixture

of delight and apprehension as the long dormant equipment whirred to life.

CLACK! CLACK! CLACK! Ali glanced up and saw storm shutters begin to unlatch on the roof. A burst of suns' rays cascaded over the drill, and it slowly turned, squeaking in protest.

Ali moved to the small opening in the door. He wanted to tell Imam right away. He also wanted Riddick to know . . . An odd *skittering* noise lifted his head.

Ali scanned the rafters. He thought he saw something move. Then the storm shutters yawned open, activated by solar panels. Relieved Ali turned back to the door, but the *skittering* sound grew louder, more agitated, like the chirping of angry birds.

As Ali looked up, his belly turned over. In the emerging light he could see the rafters were encrusted with thick black nests. When sunlight hit the first nest, it *exploded with life*.

Ali screamed and hurried to the door. He never made it.

More nests exploded, billowing into madly fluttering creatures, winged hatchlings swarming like bats in a fire, their sharp talons tearing and hacking at anything in their path. The creatures blocked Ali's exit, forcing him to veer into a dark supply room.

Ali scrambled inside and slammed the door shut. He was bleeding from some small cuts on his arm, but otherwise he was unhurt. Heart booming in the sudden quiet, Ali mumbled a prayer of thanks and crouched down, waiting for the storm outside to pass.

As he waited, the darkness around him began to rustle . . . like the frenzied scuttling of a thousand rats.

8

The party was in full swing when Riddick entered the communal room.

The pilgrims had revived the moisture recovery unit. They now had a water supply. Rashad poured the cloudy liquid into crystal goblets Paris had found somewhere. The plump merchant had also rehung a fallen Thanksgiving garland, giving the dusty room a festive touch.

Riddick was the last one to get water. There was a dark layer of sediment at the bottom of his goblet, but nothing tasted finer.

"And for this, our gift of drink, we give thanks in the name of the Prophet Mohammed," Imam intoned, raising his goblet. "And in the name of his father, Allah the compassionate and the all-merciful."

The Muslim pilgrims murmured their amens, while the others lifted their glasses. All except Riddick. He sipped his water slowly, letting it wash over the bit sores inside his mouth. He was aware of Johns' watchful eyes but he had other things in mind.

Like Fry. Riddick found her extremely attractive. Perhaps they'd find some time to explore their chemistry, Riddick thought, if they ever managed to get off the planet alive. Something very lethal lived here. And it didn't like tourists.

"Perhaps we should toast our hosts," Paris offered grandly. "Who were these people anyway? Miners?"

"Look like geologists," Shazza corrected. "Advance team, moves around from rock to rock."

Company locusts, consuming everything in their path, Riddick thought, his eyes still on Fry.

Johns squinted at Shazza. "Musta crapped out here, huh?"

"But why'd they leave their ship?" Audrey asked.

No one spoke. It was a question they weren't prepared to deal with. Because the answer was a skull-fuck, Riddick reflected. He'd seen how Zeke got taken. One second he was digging, the next he was dog meat.

He glanced at Imam. The Muslim was staring at an unclaimed water goblet on the table.

"Well, it's not really a ship," Johns said finally, giving Audrey a paternal smile. "It's just a space skiff. Disposable really . . ."

"Like an emergency life raft, right?" Paris said hopefully.

"Sure," Shazza assured him. "Coulda had a real drop-ship take them off-planet." She grinned at Audrey. "Long gone."

Paris raised his goblet. "A toast to their ghosts, then."

The others lifted their glasses. Except for Riddick.

"Didn't leave, these people," he told them flatly. "Whatever got Zeke got them. They're all dead."

The survivors glared at him as if he'd just urinated in church.

Riddick shrugged. "Why do you think they left their clothes on the lines? Pictures on the walls?"

"Maybe they had weight limits," Shazza snapped, balling her fists. "You don't know."

"I know you don't uncrate your fucking emergency skiff unless there's a fucking emergency."

"Fucking right." Audrey said, gazing at him with adoration.

"Rag it, Riddick," Johns warned. "Nobody wants your theories on . . ."

Fry turned to Riddick. "So what happened? Where are they, then?"

Riddick smiled. At least she and the little girl were willing to face reality—or take a peek at it, anyway. He looked over at Imam who was strangely quiet. The man was at the window, scanning outside.

Imam half-turned. "Has anyone seen the young one? Ali?"

Riddick glanced at Audrey. "Has anyone

checked the coring room?" he suggested.

As if in answer a faint human scream drifted up like smoke.

"Ali . . ." Imam muttered, hurrying to the door.

As the others ran toward the coring room, Riddick moved calmly around the table and drank their water . . .

Imam and Johns were the first to find the chained door. Johns racked his shotgun and fired, blasting the hinges. Imam hit the door with his shoulder and it caved in. They stumbled inside.

Empty. The dust-covered coring room was as still as a mausoleum. Behind them, Paris peered inside then carefully entered. He looked at Imam, who shrugged and began circling the large drilling chamber. Without warning the drill began to turn. Paris jumped back, heart pounding and sweat oozing through his clothes. Then he saw the solar shutters on the ceiling and realized the drill was on automatic. Even so, he remained motionless, warpick pressed against his chest.

Imam heard a noise. Then another. He moved to a closed door. "Ali?" he called softly. No answer. The boy could be too frightened to respond, Imam speculated. He tried again, louder. "Ali?"

Imam glanced back and saw Johns peering down the coring shaft. He grabbed the door handle and pulled.

A thick, black cloud of winged creatures flooded through the open door, squealing like rabid bats.

Driven by some sort of mass intelligence, the fluttering horde circled the room in a wave then soared high into the rafters. Then they disappeared.

At that moment, Ali emerged from the dark room, lurching unsteadily toward Imam. He was gushing blood and oily viscera from long, ragged tears across his shredded torso.

Suddenly the writhing, shrieking creatures burst from the rafters, flooding over them. Huddled on all fours, Paris watched in horrified fascination as the alien flock poured down into the coring shaft, their sharp cries fading into the bottomless silence.

As Ali collapsed at Imam's feet, he disintegrated; skin, flesh, and bone separating like slimy red banana peels. The pulsing remains oozing out were no longer human.

Imam blinked at the darkness beyond the door. *Ali stumbled into their nest*, he thought numbly. He bent over the boy's mutilated remains, trying to fight back the heaving nausea.

Behind him, Johns was edging over to the coring shaft. After sweeping the darkness below with his weapon, Johns unhooked a percussive flare from his belt. He tossed the flare into the shaft and waited, shotgun held ready.

When the flare hit bottom, it burst in flame, illuminating the oddly familiar debris, littering the floor.

Human bones. The skeletons of the missing settlers—scattered about and picked clean . . .

*   *   *

Nobody slept for the rest of the twin-sun day.

When the blue sun began to rise, the pilgrims held a prayer service. Paris and Audrey attended, while Riddick watched from a distance.

Whatever happened to Ali had nothing to do with God, Riddick thought. He saw Johns and Shazza heading over to the coring room and decided to join them.

As Johns and Shazza entered, they saw Fry was already inside. The blond captain didn't acknowledge their presence, intent on the shelves lining the walls.

"Why was this door chained up?" Shazza demanded. "Why the bloody hell would they lock themselves in like that?"

Johns moved closer to Fry. "Not sure. But tell you what, those Muslims better not be diggin' another grave out there."

Fry glanced up, but she wasn't looking at Johns.

"Other buildings weren't secure . . ."

Johns whirled. Riddick was standing in the doorway, goggled eyes sweeping the gloomy interior. "So they ran here. Heaviest doors. Thought they'd be safe inside here. But . . ." Riddick moved to the coring shaft and peered down. "Forgot to lock the cellar."

Shazza joined him at the edge of the shaft. They gazed down together at the distinctively human bones, scattered ribs dull white in the flare's ebbing glow.

"So that's what come of me Zeke?" Her harsh

whisper echoed down the shaft. She looked at Riddick, lips curling like an aroused predator. "An' *you* saw it. You was right there. *You* were tryin' to kill him, too."

"Not necessarily," Riddick said calmly. "Just after his O$_2$." He shrugged, goggled eyes meeting hers. "Though I noticed he tried to ghost *my* ass when he shot stranger-man instead. Stranger-man coulda' told us the fuckin' ground rules here."

Shazza couldn't deny it. She looked down the shaft, unable to meet his blank accusing stare. *Hypocrites don't last in this business*, Shazza reminded. She had done Riddick a grave wrong. Beat him bad while he was in chains.

When Shazza looked up, she saw Riddick differently. Wily, dangerous—but dead honest. She didn't believe he was a damn psycho killer. And she knew killers. Her Zeke had been one of the best.

Shazza took off her O$_2$ breather and extended it to Riddick. "Take it."

Surprise flickered over his stony features, then faded. "What, it's broken?"

Shazza shrugged and put the breather in his hand. "Still a few hits." The sudden air depletion squeezed her chest as she turned away. "Startin' to acclimate anyway."

Riddick knew better. Even cold turkey he hadn't acclimated to the sparse air. Gratefully he sucked down some pure O$_2$ and felt his ragged lungs expand like cacti in a summer rain.

Across the room Johns watched the exchange with growing unease. He didn't much like Riddick's sudden promotion from psycho scum to oxygen-breathing human.

Johns turned to Fry, voice edged with annoyance. "Let's board this up and get the hell gone. They seem to stick to the dark, so if we all stick to daylight, should be all ri—"

"Twenty-two years ago."

Fry's quiet words had an ominous tone.

"Wha . . . ?" Johns snorted, half-convinced Fry had snapped.

Fry gestured at the coring samples, arranged neatly on the shelves.

"Core samples are dated," she said carefully, as if instructing a child. "Last one is twenty-two years ago—this month."

Uncomfortable without her breather, Shazza wasn't impressed. "Yeah? So what?"

Fry hefted the dense, green rock. "I dunno," she muttered thoughtfully, as if trying to remember something. "Maybe nothing, but . . ."

Fry's intent expression softened. She looked at them, blue eyes pale with sudden clarity. "The settlement house . . ." she said, almost to herself. "The Orrery."

Only Riddick knew what she meant. The others had doubtful scowls as they trudged back to the main house.

Once there Fry went right to the solar-powered mechanical galaxy that tracked the planet's orbit around the three suns. The whirring, creaking device had a year counter. At the moment it was clicking over to 17.

Fry opened the drive box and started turning the main gear by hand, accelerating the mechanical orbits. The counter clicked monotonously: 18 . . . 19 . . . 20 . . . 21 . . .

They all saw it. At 22 it came into view.

An immense ringed world that eclipsed all the three suns and plunged their planet into darkness. Total, persistent darkness.

"Are you pullin' my prong?" Johns said in an awed voice.

Riddick took a final hit and returned the breather to Shazza. "Not ascared of the dark, are you?"

But they all were.

9

Fry was all business.

Suddenly acting like the captain everyone mistakenly thought she was, Fry crossed the compound with wide, determined strides, briskly snapping orders. ". . . Need those power cells from the crash ship right away . . ." She stopped short when they reached the skiff. "Shit—still gotta check out the hull, patch the wings . . ."

"Let's wait on those power cells," Johns suggested.

Fry thought she had heard wrong. "Wait—For what? Until it's so dark we can't find our way back to . . ."

"We're not sure when it happens," Johns said with condescending logic. "So let's not . . ."

His self-righteous arrogance touched a nerve. "Get the fucking cells over here, Johns," Fry directed. She looked at him as if examining a mental case. "What's the discussion?"

Johns glanced around covertly. Then he leaned closer. His breath reeked of alcohol. "Ever tell you how Riddick escaped?"

He let it sink in, then motioned her into the privacy of the skiff.

Johns told Riddick's story quickly and graphically, especially the details about carving his victims' body parts. But that wasn't what alarmed Fry the most.

"He can pilot?" she said incredulously. The skill required superior intelligence and intense training. It also elevated Riddick's danger potential. Once the skiff was repaired he didn't need any of them to escape—alone.

"Highjacked a prison *transport*," Johns confided. "Made a helluva good run 'fore I tracked him down."

But Fry saw the glass as half-full. "Okay, okay, maybe that's a good thing," she said hopefully. "Maybe I can use him to help with . . ."

"He also figured out how to kill the pilot, Fry."

It worked. A mental shiver smothered Fry's optimism. However, something else disturbed her. "You said we were going to trust him," Fry reminded. "You said there was a deal."

"That's what I said."

Johns met her stare, jaw clamped like a white shark, eyes challenging.

Fry didn't like what she saw. "Oh, this is a dangerous game you're playing, Johns."

"May've noticed chains don't work on this guy.

Only way we're truly safe is if he believes he's goin' free. But if he stops believin' . . ."

"You mean if he learns that you're gonna royally fuck him over."

Johns ignored her open contempt. "We bring the cells over at the last possible minute . . . when the wings are ready." He went on urgently. "When we know we're gonna launch."

Fry regarded him with undisguised amazement at his lack of basic human integrity. He was more evil than he claimed Riddick to be, Fry realized, because supposedly, Johns knew better. But through this whole ordeal the man had been obsessed with Riddick. From what she could see it was Johns who was psycho here.

"You know he hasn't harmed any of us," she said in a level voice. "Far as I can tell he hasn't even lied to us. Just stick to the deal, Johns. Let him go if that's what it—"

Johns' fingers tightened on his ever-present shotgun. "He's a murderer," he rasped, eyes bulging with sudden rage. "The law says he's gotta do his bid."

What law? Fry thought, struck by the absurdity. *Company law on an unknown planet where they were facing a nightmare death?*

But the shotgun was far from absurd, and Fry knew Johns would use it. In the name of the law, of course. She shook her head sadly and looked off. "Dancin' on razor blades here . . ."

Johns exhaled and lowered his weapon. "I won't

give him a chance to grab another ship—or slash another pilot's throat."

Fry waited for him to wave the Company flag. Instead, his point made, Johns exited the skiff and scanned the area for Riddick.

He didn't have to look far. As he descended the gangway stairs, he saw Riddick hunkered in the shade of the skiff, shaving his head with Imam's knife. Johns glanced back to the cockpit, measuring the distance.

He seemed to be out of earshot, Johns calculated warily. He gave Riddick a disappointed smile. "Thought we said no shivs."

Riddick lifted the knife, turning the blade in the sunlight. "This?" he said innocently. "This is a personal grooming appliance."

As their eyes met, chill shuddered across Johns' belly.

"Bad sign," Riddick observed, carefully guiding the blade across his skull. "Shakin' like that in this heat."

The pilgrims worked hard, shouldering a heavy roll of Vectran, the wing fabric material, all the way from the crash ship to the skiff. While waiting, Riddick constructed a crude cutting frame from metal pipes.

A short distance away Shazza repaired the Sand Cat, assisted by Audrey. But the young girl's mind wasn't on her work. She gazed at Riddick with rapt adoration, following his every move.

"You listenin', girl?" Shazza scolded. "Hand me the big wrench."

Eyes fixed on Riddick, she passed Shazza the wrench.

The pilgrims had returned with the Vectran and they helped Riddick drape the heavy fabric over the cutting frame. Then Imam climbed onto the skiff's exposed wing struts.

Riddick vanished behind the silvery Vectran. As Audrey watched, a long knife cut through the fabric and Riddick reappeared. He handed the trim to Rashad who scampered onto the skiff, balance-beamed across the wing struts, and delivered the section to Imam. The Muslim then hand-stitched the fabric to the struts like some ancient Berber rug-weaver.

Before descending for another section of fabric, Rashad paused to scan the green-tinted horizon. The blue sun was setting, but there was nothing unusual. Yet.

Inside the skiff, the cockpit hatch closed, and sealed. *So far, so good*, Fry noted, her attention focused on the monitor. The screen read HULL IN-TEGRITY TEST. Sealing the hatch had been phase one. Fry scanned the rising pressure gauges.

"Looks like we're a few shy."

Fry whirled. Riddick stood there, Imam's long blade dangling from one hand. He was staring at the depleted battery bay. "Power cells I mean," he amended.

"They're coming," she said, voice tight. "When we get the Sand Cat up."

Riddick didn't seem to hear. "Strange, not doin' a run-up on the main drive yet," he observed. "Strange . . . unless he told you the particulars of my escape."

"I got the quick-and-ugly version," Fry said, impressed by Riddick's sharp intelligence.

"And now you're worried about a repeat of history?"

"Entered our minds."

He stepped closer. "I asked what *you* thought."

"You scare me, Riddick. That's what you wanna hear, isn't it? There—I admit it. Can I get back to work now?"

Fry found the courage to turn her back on him. Riddick moved behind her and paused to study the controls. The cabin pressure was building. Any second Fry expected him to slash her throat.

"Think Johns is a do-right man?" he whispered, breath warm against the back of her neck. She leaned forward, besieged by conflicting emotions. *Did he already know? Was this a test?*

"Why, what'd you hear?" she asked, voice strained.

"Well, guess if it was trickeration he'd just X me out, huh?" Riddick speculated, mouth still brushing her neck. "Then again . . . I am worth twice as much alive."

He gently turned her around, goggled eyes reading her face. "Didn't know? Johns ain't a cop. Oh yeah, he got that nickel-slick badge, but nah—he's just another merc, and I'm just a payday. That's why he won't never kill me, see?" He bent down and whispered in her ear. "The creed, is *greed* . . ."

Unsettled by the revelation, Fry gathered herself. "Stow it, Riddick," she snapped. "We aren't going to turn on one another—no matter how hard you try."

Never mentioned turning on anybody, Riddick noted with grim amusement. He pressed closer and felt her body respond slightly. "Don't truly know *what's* gonna happen when the lights go out, Carolyn. But I do know that once the Big Dyin' starts this psycho-fuck family of ours is gonna rip itself apart. So you better find out the truth. When it all goes pitch-black—you better know exactly who's standin' behind you."

"Hull integrity . . . 100 percent" the monitor droned abruptly. Exhaling gases, the hatch hissed open.

Fry pulled away and moved quickly to the exit. Riddick didn't try to stop her.

"Oh, ask him 'bout those shakes," he suggested casually, watching her leave. "And ask why your crew-pal had to scream like that 'fore he died."

Emotions colliding like billiard balls, Fry stumbled out the door into the harsh sunlight. But as she hurried toward the compound, Riddick's last words continued to ricochet through her skull . . . *had to scream like that 'fore he died* . . .

*   *   *

The red shotgun shells were Johns's favorite.

In fact they were about the only thing he truly loved. Those fat red bullets had the power to shoot away everything corrupt, toxic, treacherous, or perverse, and propel him into a warm, cozy cocoon, where everything was as clean as new sheets, and nothing could ever touch him.

Sensual as a woman's tit, Johns thought, stroking a stack of red shells before selecting one. He went about the preparations with care, savoring each stage. First he laid out a blue disinfectant cloth and small mirror. Then he placed the syringe on the cloth and wiped it clean. Finally he popped open the shotgun shell and removed the glass ampule concealed inside. *King Morphine, monarch non grata in seven galaxies*, Johns noted fondly as he slipped the ampule into the syringe.

Peering into the mirror Johns opened his right eye wide and brought the syringe close to his eyeball. *Ultra-speed injection pierces center inner socket just above the eyeball*, Johns repeated mentally, reciting the instructions dutifully. Shooting morphine directly into the brain required close attention to detail.

He was so engrossed that he didn't hear anyone enter.

"Who are you really?"

Fry's question was like ice water. Startled, Johns glimpsed his face in the mirror, fixed between embarrassment and shameless hunger. He turned and saw her framed in the doorway.

"You're not a real cop, are you?" Fry went on, moving closer.

Johns licked his lips. "I never said I was."

"Never said you were a hype, either."

Fry's blue eyes flashed a fierce challenge as she bent down and brazenly rummaged through his open ammo bag. She came up with handfuls of red shotgun shells. Years of sweet dreams in an unfriendly universe.

"Little morphine in the morning, so what?" Johns said, recovering his composure.

Fry looked at him with seething contempt. "And here you got two mornings every day. Wow, weren't you born lucky."

"Not a problem unless you're gonna make it one . . ."

"You made it a problem when you let Owens die like that," Fry reminded, voice shaking. She opened her hand, letting the red shells spill to the floor. "When you had enough drugs to knock out an army of junkies."

Johns' eyes followed the rolling shells. "Owens was already dead. His brain hadn't caught up to that fact."

Fry's contempt escalated to sheer disgust. "Anything else we should know about you, Johns? Christ, here I am lettin' you roll dice with our lives when you . . ."

Without warning Johns caught her wrists. As Fry struggled he pulled her arms around his body, forcing her into an embrace. He pressed her hands against the small of his back. She felt something hard and leathery running along his spine. Dimly she realized what it was and stopped struggling.

Johns released her hands and turned so she could see. A thick, jagged scar zigzagged his backbone, like a purple shoelace.

"My first run-in with Riddick. Went for the sweet spot and missed. They had to leave a piece of the shiv in there," Johns added, steely eyes locking on hers. "I can feel it sometimes . . . pressin' against the cord. Feel it movin' under my skin. Like little spiders tryin' to chew their way out. So maybe the care and feeding of my nerve-ends is my business."

Bloated with self-pity but not a drop of human mercy, Fry thought, disgust brimming over into hatred. "You coulda helped—and you didn't."

Johns shrugged and began gathering the scattered shells. "Yeah. Well, look to thine own ass first. Right, Carolyn?"

He used her name like an icepick, reminding Fry that she had tried to cancel everyone's ticket to save her skin.

Through her fuming anger Fry was aware of jabbering shouts outside. The frantic Arabic was punctuated by a single English word. "*Captain!*" The Muslims were calling. "*Captain!*"

Suddenly Rashad appeared in the doorway. "Captain, quick!" he said breathlessly.

Fry shouldered past him. "I'm not your fucking captain, okay?"

She strode outside, closely followed by Rashad. Johns stayed behind long enough to wrap his brain in a silky turban of morphine before joining the others.

The survivors were gathered on a ridge, silently staring at the shimmering sky.

It looked like a drug-inspired laser-show. An immense arch curved overhead, like a black rainbow. Darkly luminous, deeply ominous, it hung over them like a funeral wreath.

They watched hypnotically, as the huge arch kept rising, inching toward the twin suns.

Shazza was the first to rouse from her trance. She grabbed Fry's shoulder and shook her awake. "If we need anythin' from the crash ship—I suggest we kick on!" Shazza declared. "That Sand Cat's solar-powered."

But as the survivors raced toward the vehicle, an enormous shadow crept across the desert . . .

Johns risked missing the bus to retrieve his shotgun shells from the main house.

He swung out the door and ran awkwardly to catch up to the Sand Cat. Riddick reached down and reeled him aboard. For a moment his face was inches from Johns's.

"Don't wanna miss this," Riddick grinned.

"Lookit!" Audrey cried. "Lookit!"

They turned back and saw the rim of a colossal planet, cresting over the horizon. Fry realized the luminous arch was actually the planet's ring. *It's happening too quick*, she realized, fear booming through her belly.

Shazza seemed to have the same thought. Her long black hair flared around her head as she stepped hard on the accelerator. The Sand Cat responded, engine whining as the vehicle bumped and rocked across the desert. When they entered the maze of giant bones Shazza didn't slow down, weaving wildly through the obstacle course. The Sand Cat hit a rough bump, spilling some percussive flares. *We need those*, Fry thought frantically, but it was too late to stop.

Behind them, the shadow was spreading across the desert as if in pursuit. Shazza kept the Cat moving, skillfully guiding the bulky vehicle through the canyon graveyard. As they roared full-throttle inside a massive ribcage, the Cat's roll-bar smashed out some low-bridge bones, showering them with sharp chips.

Finally they reached the crash ship, but the shadow had overtaken them. They all leaped off the Cat and sprinted to the cargo container.

Huffing and sweating, Paris paused to steal a look and was transfixed.

He stood rooted in stunned awe, like Lot's wife, as he watched the gigantic black planet swallow up the universe.

10

The survivors scurried for the battery
bay with the fervent urgency of ants before a storm.
Elbowing ahead, Johns yanked the first power cell
from its socket and began dragging it over the deck.
Riddick yanked a second cell and swung it onto his
shoulder. Muscles oiled with sweat, Riddick shot
the struggling Johns a kiss-my-ass grin as he
passed.

Ignoring his stampeding heartbeat, Johns awkwardly shouldered the leaden cell and stumbled after Riddick.

Shazza wheeled the Cat closer to the ship. Riddick dumped the first cell onto the vehicle, Johns
the second. They were racing each other—and the
rapidly approaching eclipse. Everyone kept working feverishly. Fry loaded cutting torches onto the
Cat and went back to help Audrey with a case of
food.

As Riddick emerged, hauling another cell, he

glanced up. The planet's dark ring already blotted out the yellow sun, creating a surreal orange and black twilight. The red sun's glare highlighted the nearby pinnacles and they loomed like witches' hats against a Halloween sky.

Last call, Riddick observed ruefully.

"Don't stop! Don't stop!" Fry shouted.

But as Riddick eased the heavy cell onto the Cat, he knew they wouldn't make it. Their daylight was almost used up.

It was as if God was closing the blinds. And as the orange sky darkened, a faint, high-pitched squealing drifted across the dusk.

"Keep working. Don't stop!" Fry warned.

But Paris couldn't resist. He squinted in the direction of the sound.

The plump dealer sniffed the air like a point dog and saw the pinnacles standing in the distance. *Yes*, Paris decided, *the sounds are definitely coming from the pinnacles*. Pleased with his little discovery, he lifted the case of liquor.

Before Paris reached the Cat, the giant ring began blotting out the red sun. Only the fading halos of orange light around the pinnacles kept the night at bay.

Suddenly a second darkness swept over the survivors. They all stopped, heads turning toward the growing, high-pitched clamor. When Fry located the source her legs turned to water.

It billowed out of the pinnacles like writhing black smoke. Backlit by orange coronal light it seemed to be thick volcanic ash spewing from the hollow peaks. But after a few seconds Fry realized these were living things. Newly hatched creatures squealing in delight over their first nightfall.

"Jesus," Johns growled. "How many can there . . . ?"

His words trailed off as the hatchlings kept coming in waves, blotting out what little light remained. *Thank God they're moving away from us,* Fry thought, gaping at the dense black clouds of hatchlings boiling across the sky like thunderheads.

It was wishful thinking.

As she watched, one huge wave of creatures cleaved away from another, and peeled back toward them, screeching wildly as they came.

"Just a suggestion," Paris offered, backing toward the ship, "but perhaps we should flee."

"Cargo hold!" Fry yelled. "Everyone in the cargo hold! Lesgo! Lesgo! Lesgo!"

The survivors scrambled for the safety of the cargo container. When Fry reached the metal hold she turned back and saw Riddick and Shazza still coming. Shazza had trouble running and Riddick was dragging her along. Just behind them the squealing, twisting torrent of hatchlings was descending like a tornado.

Riddick and Shazza hit the dirt an instant before the screeching wave swooped low, skimming inches over their heads. They seemed to suck everything from the air, leaving nothing for Shazza to breathe. She shut her eyes tight, face pressed against the alien sand and lungs swelling as if she were underwater.

Riddick, on the other hand, was fascinated. He lay on his back, staring at the roiling, shrieking mass above his head with no more fear than a kid looking up at the stars. Until he decided to experiment.

Probing very carefully, Riddick eased his bone shiv into the black swirl above him. Instantly something slapped at it. When Riddick pulled it back the blade was whittled down to a jagged nub. *It's like a river of razor blades*, he realized, heart quickening.

Shazza's heartbeat was galloping like a mad horse. She lay huddled against Riddick, fists clenched and skin prickling with a thousand alien species of vermin. Jovian slime worms, Venusian snapping tarantulas, Ovidian vampire snakes, Magellan earwigs . . . every crawling, oozing, loathsome life-form imaginable was swarming over her skin.

Nerves frayed like violin strings, Shazza heard a discordant screech inside her skull, like chalk on a slate—and snapped. She whipped a panicky look at the nearby ship. *Not that far*, she told herself, mind screeching with terror as she wormed toward the cargo hold.

Abruptly, the gibbering swarm dissolved. In the sudden quiet, Shazza lifted her head. They were gone. Tentatively she got to her feet . . .

Audrey saw the whole thing from the cargo

hold. The black swirl rose up and circled, as if lost. A moment later Shazza awkwardly stood up.

Audrey waved her arms and shouted, "Tell her to stay there. Stay down, Shazza! JUST STAY DOWN!"

Riddick extended a hand to stop her, but Shazza started running toward the ship.

"NO, NO!" Audrey shrieked as the dark cloud gathered above Shazza's stumbling form. *"NO! NO! NO!"*

Shazza heard too late. She half-turned as the screaming cloud enveloped her—then vanished. Audrey stood stunned at the mouth of the hold, peering out at the silent emptiness.

Without warning a squealing torrent blew past the doors. Horrified, Audrey caught a last glimpse of Shazza whirling in the center of the howling storm, her body shredded into bloody kite tails, before she disappeared into the lowering darkness.

The others saw it, too. Reflexively they shrank back from the mouth of the hold. But Audrey couldn't move. Paralyzed with terror, she watched helplessly as Riddick stirred, checked right and left as if about to cross a busy street, and slowly got to his feet.

Too slowly, Audrey thought. She tried to shout but nothing came.

Clapping his hands clean, Riddick strolled to the hold like a man on vacation.

A familiar clicking rose up behind him. Fry

moved to the doors. She knew that sound better than anyone.

CLICKETY-CLICK . . . CLICKETY-CLICK . . .

As the sound grew louder, Riddick bent to pick something up. It was Shazza's breather. Fry looked behind him and saw the pinnacles crumbling—as if being eaten from within.

The only light remaining was a narrow strip of orange flame shooting up from the massive rim of the ascending planet. The falling darkness, disintegrating pinnacles, and relentless *clicking* came to an eerie crescendo as Riddick suddenly broke into a flat-out sprint—as if pursued by an unseen predator.

Just as Riddick reached the hold, the narrow red corona flickered out like a candle, and the world plunged into perpetual night.

At the mouth of the hold, Riddick lifted his goggles, and looked out with his jaguar eyes. Riddick's night vision gave him a clearer image of the creatures emerging from their collapsed nests. He could crudely trace their features: large, mammalian predators with hammerheads and vicious talons. They launched themselves into the night sky, leathery wings spread, gliding, clicking, searching . . .

Like bats, Riddick realized, *clicking for echo location . . . Sounding out a world they haven't inhabited for twenty-two years . . .*

"What is it?" Fry asked, watching his face. "What's happening?"

Riddick lowered the goggles over his eyes. "Like I said. Ain't me you gotta worry about."

The hold's vaultlike doors boomed shut. Locked inside, with only their handlights, the survivors huddled like Neanderthals in a cave, listening to the yowls of the circling sabertooths.

Audrey stubbornly resisted the lockdown, hoping for a miracle. "What if . . . what if she's still out there . . ." she insisted, ". . . still alive?"

"Well," Johns rumbled. "I don't want to jump to conclusions here . . . but remember that boneyard? These just might be the very same fuckers that killed every other living thing on this hell-planet, okay? Chances of Shazza knockin' on that door soon just about zero squared."

Fry nodded agreement. "I saw the cut marks on the bones," she said gently. "Wasn't a natural die-off . . ."

Suddenly, Imam moved to the door as if he'd heard something. As he pressed his ear against the door, the others gathered around him, their own ears tuned like radar. They all heard the *clicking* sweep restlessly past, just outside the door.

"Why do they do that—make that sound?" Audrey demanded.

Imam gave her a patient smile. "Perhaps the way they see," he suggested. "With sound, reflecting back."

"Echo location," Fry said. "That's what it is."

More clicking cut across the gloom. The survivors whipped their lights around to find . . . nothing. Only a partially open container, about halfway down the tunnel-like hold.

The survivors glanced fearfully at each other, then at Fry. *How the fuck could one get in here?* they seemed to ask.

"Breach in the hull," Fry suggested, voice tight. "I dunno," she added, eyes locked on the open door.

The *clicking* seemed to come closer. Fry and the others looked at Johns. Slowly he realized they expected him to check it out. "I'd rather piss glass," he declared.

"Well, you've got the big gauge," Riddick pointed out.

Johns lifted the weapon. "Wanna rag your fat mouth?"

"Maybe it's just their beads again," Fry offered hopefully. "Imam, are you still—"

"No, no, no," Imam protested, covering his prayer beads. "I do not believe—"

"C'mon, man," Johns growled, "you're drivin' everybody bugfuck with those things. Why don't you just lose the goddamn . . ."

The *clicking* sound grew louder, closely followed by the crash of toppling cargo.

Riddick smiled at Johns. "Big beads."

Taking a deep breath, Johns cocked his weapon and edged toward the open container. Leading with his shotgun he leaned around the door and fired blindly. Something screeched . . . then was quiet.

Johns eased his light around the door and saw them. Two shredded, bat-winged lizards smeared across the floor like road kill.

Without warning something swept down at his head, swinging a curved talon like a scythe. The talon caught his shotgun and it discharged. In the fragmented flash Johns glimpsed an image that burned into his mind. Curved teeth inside ravenous jaws, blank, liquid eyes, and strangely pulsing ears that throbbed and twitched with constant hungry movement . . .

Hungry for my ass, Johns thought wildly as he jerked back behind the door and slammed it shut. But as Johns backed away he noticed more cracks in their little shelter.

"Very big beads," Johns declared, when he rejoined the others. "Need to find someplace more secure."

His report roused Paris from his terrified stupor. Deprived of alcohol, he'd hit the wall. *This is real*, he thought, skull screaming with fear. *They're inside with us.* The plump dealer clutched his warpick and began pulling at the main door, ready to flee into the night.

"Not staying here another—"

Fry lunged and yanked him back before he could open the door. "Christ, you don't know what's out there!"

"I know what's *in here!*" Paris quavered, struggling weakly.

Suddenly the *clicking* sounds erupted all around

them. Imam opened a door connecting to the other containers. "This way," he said. "Hurry please." Rashad and Hasan slipped inside, closely followed by Paris and the others.

Imam made sure everyone was inside before slamming the doors shut.

At first the only sounds in the dark, cramped space was the hiss of their breathers. Then the scratching noises clawed through the quiet. Johns pulled out a cutting torch and fumbled with the knob. As the torch flared he adjusted the gasses to emit a wide arc of light that illuminated the metal door. And he saw what caused the scratching.

Sharp, bladelike talons were probing the door joints; prying, raking, picking with single-minded intensity. The survivors shrank away from the door. The hairs on the back of Audrey's neck prickled. She glanced up and screamed.

Fingerlike talons were stabbing down through a metal grate just above their heads. Everyone ducked low. Imam beamed his light at the grate in time to glimpse saw-toothed lizard tails snaking away into the darkness.

Quiet fell over them like a blanket. Johns lifted his cutting torch, throwing light around him and saw Riddick, hands crossed over his eyes.

"Can you do sumpin' else with that?" he snarled. " 'Sides holdin' it in my fucking face?"

Johns turned away. He compressed the flame to a blue-white point, and began cutting through the common wall to the other containers. The moment the torch began slicing metal, a violent rattling noise filled the chamber.

Imam skimmed his light across the ceiling and saw a large grate shaking furiously as if something was pounding on it, trying to smash it. Behind them the talons attacking the door were sawing it apart— literally *tearing it open*.

Working intently Johns burned an outline on the wall and kicked it open. Audrey speed-crawled between his legs and found herself in the freezer unit. The chaos was worse in there, with the *rattling, scratching, clicking* suddenly amplified. As the others crawled inside the scuttling on the metal ceiling seemed to pursue them. Suddenly a pressure tube overhead exploded. Sharp talons jabbed wildly through the white cloud of ultracold gas filling the chamber. More bladelike talons cut through the soft pressure tubs, spewing fumes everywhere.

Shivering, Riddick peered through the freezing gas and saw Johns burning another exit in the wall. Then it dawned.

We're being herded, he realized with a flurry of panic. But it was too late.

Johns cut through the wall into an oversized container. When Riddick stepped inside he saw there was no ceiling grate, and it was large enough to enable them to move comfortably. Immediately Hasan and Rashad started muscling heavy cargo in front of the hole.

Riddick stood where he was, circling slowly. He sensed something was wrong.

Johns heaved a crate against the opening and glared at Riddick. "What union you belong to?" he rasped. "How about a fucking hand?"

Riddick ignored him. He was looking at the pepper-shot pockmarks on the wall with growing suspicion. He moved away from the gathered hand-lights into the darkness.

"Where is he?" Audrey whispered urgently, the first to notice.

Riddick turned and felt something squish under his foot, something soft and oily. He slipped off his goggles.

It was a dead hatchling, its bat-lizard body ripped open by a shotgun.

Johns' shotgun. An icy finger of fear jabbed his belly. *We've been herded back where we started*, he thought numbly.

Then he sensed it. The energy. Slowly, very slowly, Riddick lifted his face to the darkness above him—and saw it. A live hatchling squatted atop some cargo. Its fanged jaws were devouring something clutched in its talons.

As Riddick stared he realized it was one of the hatchlings Johns had shot.

Vicious fuckers eat their own, he noted with disgust. As if stung by the insult, the creature paused. Cocking its hammer-shaped head, it swept the area with inquisitive *clicks*. At the same time its ears twitched incessantly.

Then the creature's ears went rigid.

Alarmed by the alien sounds Fry peered through

the gloom and spotted Riddick. She started closer,
then stopped short, belly churning with raw terror.

Riddick was in a stare-down with an alien predator. Jaguar eyes gleaming, he stood motionless as
the creature's razor tipped wings enfolded him in
an unholy embrace . . .

11

Hasan was intent on blocking the burn hole.

The burly pilgrim stacked a heavy crate then went off in search of another. He didn't bother with his handlight as he rounded the corner. First mistake.

A steely grip squeezed Hasan's skull like a vise.

"*Don't*," Riddick whispered, "*move*."

Hasan rolled his eyes and saw the creature perched in front of them. His limbs went limp. If Riddick didn't have him in a headlock, Hasan would have collapsed.

But Riddick wasn't concerned about the creature in front of them. It was the hatchling descending from the ceiling that had him worried.

This one wanted to touch.

Riddick held his breath, hands tight around the pilgrim's head. He kept his gaze fixed on the creature in front of him, but Riddick was uncomfortably aware of the bony talon probing the top of his skull. To make things even more uncomfortable, the creature facing him folded its wings tighter. Closed inside, Riddick's senses were assailed by a foul stench that curdled his belly with nausea. The *clicking* became louder.

When the talon stroked Hasan's head, he wet himself, urine soaking his socks and running over his shoes in a foaming yellow stream of pure fear. A shudder convulsed his body and he felt a blinding pain as Riddick's hands squeezed his skull tighter. The *clicking* sound rose up in his brain.

Unable to breathe he began to lose consciousness . . .

Riddick remained rock-still as more blade-sharp talons descended, and began moving over his body like surgical instruments. One talon test-sliced Riddick's shirt, grazing his skin.

Then he heard Fry's voice. "Riddick?"

Bad time, sweetheart, he noted grimly. He managed a two-word reply.

"Keep. Burning."

Johns heard him and understood. *This is the open container*. Frantically, he started burning through the next wall.

"Hasan?" Imam called out.

But the pilgrim couldn't answer. Reeling from the stench, and convulsed with terror, he wheezed breathlessly as a talon stroked his chest. The talon lightly test-sliced Hasan's skin, drawing blood. As the blood welled up, all clicking ceased.

Instinctively Hasan knew why the noise had stopped. Cold dread shriveled his genitals. Without thinking, he bolted.

Second mistake. Game over.

Focused on the baleful eyes of the creature in front of him, Riddick felt the pilgrim wrench free. "No!" he yelled as Hasan yanked apart the leathery wings and began running.

He didn't get two steps before the predators were on him. Hasan vanished behind a blurred fury of raw hunger. Even his death scream was cut short, devoured by the ravenous intensity of ripping talons and fanged jaws.

Glimpsing a window of opportunity, Riddick jumped. But the moment he moved, another predator loomed up, blocking his path.

Reflexively Riddick darted around a stack of cargo and sprinted for the escape hatch. But as the screeching predator swooped after him Riddick knew he'd never make it.

A sudden glaring explosion blinded him. Howling in pain, Riddick stumbled forward, bony talons raking his neck.

As he dove through the hatch, Fry's light beamed past Riddick's shoulder, hitting the raging creature behind him. Amazingly, the light produced a similar reaction.

Screeching, the predator scrambled back.

Fry stood stunned, the light beam drilling through the empty darkness. *Was it* really *me that stopped it?*

In answer, a shotgun blasted past her ear. Startled, Fry dropped the light. As she scrambled after it, Johns pushed her aside and began shooting shadows. Jacked up on primal fear, he fired round after round.

"Stop it!" Fry yelled. "STOP IT!"

Finally he stopped. " 'Sokay, 'sokay, I killed it," he assured breathlessly.

The others exchanged knowing glances. Johns had snapped.

Suddenly a carcass slammed wetly to the floor, like some huge black manta ray with thorny wings. Everyone leaped back in a quick splash pattern.

"Christ," Paris said in a hushed voice. "He did kill one."

Fry retrieved her light and beamed it on the carcass. Wherever the light touched it, the flesh charred and bubbled, sending up fumes.

"There . . ." she said. *"Look!"*

"Like the light is scalding it," Paris affirmed, his confidence returning.

"It hurts them," Fry announced triumphantly. "Light actually *hurts them*!"

A sudden chittering frenzy swept out of the darkness as the voracious predators fought for what scraps remained of their prey.

"Is that . . . Hasan?" Imam's question hovered above the nightmare sounds.

Johns moved first. "We'll burn a candle for him later," he muttered, igniting his torch. "C'mon."

*   *   *

Audrey was born again.

It had happened exactly twice before. The first when she'd emerged, wailing in protest, from her mother's womb. And the second when she stowed away on the space freighter.

Only this time around she wasn't so tough. This time she was helpless; a frightened little ewe, lost in an alien slaughterhouse. And it had the others worried. Until now, the runaway's brash courage had been an inspiration—as if her innocent valor could save them.

But the bubble had finally burst. For all her bravado, Audrey was just a child.

Poor kid can't handle the horror, Fry reflected, hugging her knees. *Nobody can.*

It was true. The survivors had taken refuge in a small container, and sat huddled in the protective glow of a single lantern. To prevent the group from falling into apathy, Fry roused herself and called for a weapons check.

"I've got one cutting torch, one handlight here," she droned, like an auctioneer. "At least one more in the cabin."

"Spirits," Paris offered, his courage refueled by a slug of cognac. He patted the case he'd just discovered. "Anything over forty-five proof burns well."

"How many bottles?" When Paris hesitated, Fry added, "If you got a receipt?"

"Not sure," Paris sighed. "Ten?" He kept one

bottle for medicinal purposes and pushed the case toward her.

Fry glanced at Johns. "And you have some flares. So all right, maybe we have enough light."

Something in her tone alerted Johns. "Enough for what?"

She turned and regarded him with steady blue eyes as if the answer was obvious.

It was. But Johns didn't like it. "Oh lady, if you're in your right mind, I pray you go insane."

Fry ignored him, appealing to the others. "We can stick to the plan," she announced, eyes sweeping the small circle. "If we get four cells back to the skiff—we can lose this boneyard."

Four power cells, Paris thought ruefully, *might as well be a hundred*. He shook his head. "I hate to kill a beautiful theory with an ugly fact—but that Sand Cat won't run at night."

"We'll have to carry the cells," Fry declared. "Drag them, whatever it takes."

The suggestion drew a troubled silence. The idea of hauling heavy cells through the raging death-gauntlet outside had a suicidal ring. But both Imam and Riddick noticed the lantern on the floor had become a shade dimmer.

Audrey slowly lifted her head. "You mean . . ." She searched for the word, "*tonight*? With all those *things* still out there?"

For once Paris agreed with the little urchin. "Oh sure—why not? Sounds like a hoot."

"Back up," Johns snapped. He pointed at Fry.

"How long can this *tonight* last? Few more minutes, few more hours . . . ?"

Fry glanced at Imam, who shrugged. He had done preliminary calculations on the Orrery. The mechanical planetary system was both intricate and simple. As a mathematician and engineer, Imam grasped the principle. But he didn't have time to work out the details. "I had the impression . . . from the model . . . that the two planets were moving as one."

He looked around. The faces were still hopeful. "That there would be . . . a lasting darkness," he explained regretfully.

"The sun's gotta come out sometime," Johns scoffed, jaw set in a stubborn scowl. "And if these . . . beasts really are phobic about light, we just sit here till dawn."

Fry shrugged and turned away. "I'm sure that's what someone else said. Locked inside that coring room."

It was a persuasive image. Fry, Riddick, Imam, Rashad; all eyes swung back to Audrey. Johns pounced on their concern like a politician.

"Look, we gotta think about everyone now—the kid especially. How scared is she gonna be out there?"

Fry felt like throwing up. "Oh, don't use her like that!"

"Like what?"

Innocence wasn't his strong suit, Fry noted. "For a smokescreen," she said, voice barbed with contempt. "Just deal with your own fears."

Johns' face reddened. "Hey, why don't you just rag your hole for two seconds—and let me come up with a plan that doesn't involve mass suicide, okay?"

Fry waited two long seconds before she spoke. "How much do you weigh, Johns?"

"What the hell's it matter?"

"How much?"

"Seventy-nine kilos—why?"

"Because you are seventy-nine kilos of gutless white meat. And *that's* why you can't come up with a better plan."

Johns had killed men for less. But as he swung his shotgun Riddick stepped between them. Hands shaking with fury, Johns prodded the underside of Riddick's chin with the weapon.

"Think about that reward, Johns," Riddick reminded calmly.

Johns' finger tightened on the trigger. "I'm willing to take a cut in pay."

"How about a cut in your gut?"

The question pierced his mindless rage. Johns looked down and saw Riddick's shiv angled against his belly, poised for the quick slice that would spread his intestines across the floor. *The blast might knock him back*, Johns calculated, still nose-to-nose with the goggled killer.

"Please," Imam implored, stretching out a hand between them. "This solves nothing . . . Please."

Soon, very soon, Johns promised silently, lowering his shotgun. As he stepped back there was a collective intake of breath.

Fry knelt beside Audrey. "They're afraid of our light," she explained gently. "That means we don't have to be so afraid of them."

Imam joined them. "Are you certain you can find your way back to the skiff?" he asked quietly. "Even in the dark?"

"No, I'm not," Fry admitted. "But *he* can . . ."

They all turned. She was pointing at Riddick.

Fry mixed her cutter for maximum flame. Cracking open the main door, she pushed the cutter outside and swept it around. Satisfied it was clear, she stepped through the crack. One by one the others followed.

They moved like some multilegged insect, huddled together inside a protective halo of light, as they slowly crossed open ground. All around them the primal sounds grew louder, more insistent, as if the hatchlings were massed just beyond the glow, waiting ravenously for them to falter.

Fry tried not to listen. When they neared the main cabin, she glanced back.

"Riddick."

Without hesitation Riddick separated from the group and stepped into the blackness. Removing his goggles, he peered inside the cabin. Lots of wreckage, but no sign of life.

"Looks clear," he muttered.

Impatiently, Johns shouldered him aside and

crawled into the cabin. The moment his handlight beamed in, a shadow fluttered to life and buzz-sawed over his head. Squealing in panic, the creature shot through the door, into the darkness.

"Fuck me!" Johns shouted. "You said *'clear'!"*

"Said, *'looks* clear,' " Riddick corrected.

Johns remained pressed against the wall, ready to blast anything that moved.

"Well, what's it look like now?"

Riddick made a few tongue-clicks in the dark. "Looks clear."

He could feel Johns' anger flaring. So could Fry. She stepped inside before he boiled over. "Just get the goddamn lights on."

Riddick found the switch. The others scrambled aboard as the main lights flickered on. As they went about their tasks with renewed energy, Imam was reminded of what fire meant to the cavemen. How desolate and wretched existence had been before some bright ape found the spark.

The cabin's illumination seemed to recharge the survivors' spirits. Rashad came up with a clever improvement on Paris' misting umbrellas, and made the adjustments. Audrey helped, filling the reservoirs with high-octane cognac. Meanwhile, Riddick powered up the system lights, then yanked a cell from a battery bay.

The tricky part was loading up the sled outside. The moment Riddick stepped into the darkness he felt them closing around him. He heaved the cell aboard then hurried back for another.

Imam dumped the dead O_2 canisters and made sure all the breathers carried fresh units. He handed one to Riddick who nodded thanks, sucked in some fresh oxygen, then swung a power cell onto his shoulder and headed outside.

Finally it was time to yank the last cell. *Time to run the gauntlet*, Johns brooded. Reluctantly he moved to the exit. An icy shudder stopped him in his tracks. Johns fumbled with a pocket, and found a red morphine shell. Just the feel of it in his hand dispelled the sickness scratching at his belly. He stroked it lovingly with his thumb.

"Ready, Johns," Fry said, behind him.

He palmed the morphine shell and turned. "He'll lead you over the first cliff. You know that, don't you?"

Fry was fed up with Johns' paranoid obsession with Riddick. "We're just burnin' light here," she said impatiently.

Johns stood his ground, "You give him the cells and the ship and he will leave you all out there to die."

His harsh whine was like a broken record, digging into her brain. Fry snapped. "I don't get it, Johns. What is so goddamn valuable in your life that you're worried about losing? Huh? Is there anything else *at all* you think about? Besides your next spike?"

She pushed past him and left the cabin. Seconds later the lights faded out.

Still fuming, Johns stood in the dark and loaded his shotgun. *We're all going on a death march, bitch*, he ranted silently, shoving a shell in the chamber. *And Riddick is the Pied Piper.*

12

A fiery cloud blossomed like a blue
flower in the darkness.

Rashad grinned in delight. His little invention
worked. He'd placed a large burning wick in the
center of Paris's misting umbrella. When the cloud
of alcohol blew over the wick it burst into flame,
creating a fireball.

Now the caravan had two umbrella torches, their
fabric already burned away by the fireballs belching up into the endless night.

Quickly they saddled up. Imam chained himself
into the first harness of the sled. Beside him Johns
fumbled with the second harness. Riddick came up
to help Johns with his chains. As the goggled outlaw locked Johns into the harness both men recognized the irony of the prisoner chaining his
captor.

"Keep the light going," Fry instructed the group.

"That's all we have to do to live through this. Just keep your light burn—"

Suddenly a multi-colored spray of holiday lights blinked on like a fat Christmas tree. Fry made out the pasty white face inside. Paris. He had swaddled himself in vintage Christmas lights powered by a belt-pack battery.

Ingenious . . . but pathetic, Fry thought.

Paris read her expression. "What?" he said indignantly. "You said the more light the better, so . . ." He glared at the others defensively. "Well, someone can stand real close to me if they want."

His offer was met by stony silence. Paris stamped his foot in exasperation.

"What?" he demanded, turning to Fry. "You think I should give them up, so someone *else* can . . ."

Fry shrugged. "Keep 'em. You'll need every watt back there."

"Back there?" Paris repeated, eyes blinking rapidly. "Back where?"

"You're the the tail-gunner," Fry said with a tight smile. She hefted John's shotgun and shoved Paris behind the sled. "Thanks for volunteering."

Actually this ridiculous fop and Johns are a lot alike, Fry reflected, moving to the head of the pack. *Both self-obsessed assholes.* Then there was Riddick. Despite everything, she kept remembering Johns's warning.

Riddick stood at the front of the caravan. He had looped a handlight over his neck and down his back, so it shone as a beacon. He nodded at Fry as she approached.

"Be runnin' about ten paces ahead," he told her tersely. "I want light on my back—but not in my eyes. And check your cuts. Those things know our blood scent now."

Fry glanced down and saw Audrey nearby. The little girl's face was wooden with fright. Fry prayed she had made the right decision.

"Riddick," she said hurriedly. "I was thinking we should make some kind of deal. Just in case, you know, this actually . . ."

"Had it with deals."

The four words rang in Fry's skull like alarm bells. "But I just wanted to say—"

"Nobody's gonna turn a murderer loose," he said flatly. "I fuckin' know better."

Fry was worried. *If he doesn't expect to go free*, she speculated darkly, *why save us?*

"Been a long time since anyone's trusted me," Riddick said. He lowered his voice and leaned very close. "That's somethin' right there."

Fry could feel his animal heat. "We can, can't we?" she asked, voice husky. "Trust you?"

Riddick smiled and lifted his goggles. "Actually—that's what I've been asking myself."

For a terrible moment Fry stared into his shimmering jaguar eyes. Then he turned away. Fry watched him stride into the blackness, still wondering if she'd made a fatal mistake.

*   *   *

Running point, goggles off, eyes flashing through the darkness, Riddick felt almost free. But his tuned senses were acutely aware of the restless shapes just at the edge of his vision. They hovered close, waiting for the slightest mistake.

The procession resembled an illuminated circus train. Imam and Johns pulled the sled, their hand-lights sweeping ahead. Rashad manned the first side-guard position, carrying an umbrella torch. Fry and Audrey took second side-guard, their umbrella spewing fireballs.

Swathed in colored lights like some electric clown, Paris stumbled along at rear point, jabbing his cutting torch at every shadow.

Fry was reassured by the Sand Cat tracks underfoot. Riddick was retracing their mad flight to beat the darkness. But she couldn't help being unnerved by the relentless sounds all around them, like thousands of snapping teeth.

They had marched about two kilometers when Fry noticed that the Sand Cat tracks had vanished. With a sinking feeling she moved ahead, searching for the familiar waffle tracks that led to the skiff.

"So you noticed, too?"

Fry turned and saw Johns' knowing smirk. She paused and scanned the darkness ahead. "Riddick," she called anxiously. "Riddick!"

The caravan ground to a halt. Everyone sucked hard on their breathers, like pacifiers, as they clustered inside the light.

Suddenly Riddick emerged from the blackness.

"Where are the Sand Cat tracks?" Fry demanded. "Why aren't we still following them?"

Riddick squinted past her. "Saw something I didn't like."

"Such as?"

"Hard to tell sometimes, even for me . . . but looked like a bunch of those big boys chewing each other's gonads off." He smiled at her, eyes flashing like knives. "Thought we'd give it the swerve."

Paris approached them, mouth open in frightened disbelief. "*Swerve . . . around what?*"

The *clicking* sounds swirled closer, ending the discussion.

"Let's move!" Fry shouted. She glanced at Audrey. "Just a detour," she assured. "He'll get us there."

Audrey shrugged. She trusted Riddick. It was the others that worried her.

"Can we switch?" Paris whined.

Distracted, Fry didn't understand. "What? Switch what?"

"I think I twisted my ankle running backward like that," he said accusingly. "And now I'm not sure I can . . ." Aware that everyone was giving him disgusted looks, Paris paused and appealed to Fry. "Okay, that's a lie. I just don't want to be alone back there anymore. If you could just give me a few minutes up front here . . ."

Johns didn't like it. *Bad luck, like changing seats in a poker game*. "She's the pilot," he growled at Paris. "She should stay close to the cells."

Paris drew himself up. "Oh? So I'm disposable?"

"I'll switch. I'll switch!" Fry said quickly, alarmed by the shadows gliding past their circle of light. "Christ, just get this train *moving!*"

The illuminated caravan trundled on through the rustling blackness.

Walking side-guard Paris actually started to relax a bit. *At least there's only one exposed side*, he noted smugly. Unfortunately the infernal clicking was never out of earshot. The sound grated on his nerves. He swilled some cognac and looked up. A weak fireball coughed from his umbrella torch. Paris checked his reservoir. Almost empty.

"Reloading," Paris called out, "reloading."

Audrey moved to fetch a fresh bottle from the sled. Without thinking she strayed from the light of Fry's fireball. The moment she stepped into shadow a high-velocity *clicking* pierced the darkness like an incoming missile.

The sound jolted Imam's instincts. He ducked his harness and dove for the little girl. As Imam pulled her down, bony talons slashed like white scythes—*and shattered his light*.

Fry lifted the gun, but Johns was faster. He grabbed the shotgun from her hand and blasted the shadows above Audrey's head. Rashad's light darted through the darkness around Imam. Holding the torch aloft, Fry beamed her own handlight at them.

"Please . . . have we been cut?" Imam asked, checking his hands and feet. "Can somebody bring a light and tell me . . ."

On the other side of the sled, Paris found himself momentarily isolated. Abruptly his torch went out. He still had the Christmas lights, but the smothering darkness made him nervous. As he shuffled to the sled for an alcohol refill, he tripped over his own wires.

And suddenly he was in total darkness. The Christmas lights had gone out.

Frantically his pudgy fingers went over the warm bulbs trying to track down the loose one. "Oh shit . . . ohshitohshitohshit . . ."

A heavy shape bumped his leg. Reflexively Paris grabbed the spot and felt something warm and sticky. *Blood*, he realized numbly. Then his heartbeat froze.

The clicking had stopped.

"Sweet Jesus!" Paris shrieked. "WILL YOU GET ME SOME LIGHT OVER HERE!"

Fry whipped her light toward his voice.

"OVER HERE!" Paris screamed, crawling awkwardly toward the sled. All around him the night had claws, tearing pieces from his living flesh. Light swept the ground a few feet away, but as he cried out a talon ripped his throat open. Gurgling blood, Paris tumbled into a boiling cauldron of red-hot razor blades.

Fry caught a glimpse of a shredded leg before it was snatched away by a swooping blur. Their light beams lanced fitfully through the darkness, but it was too late. Paris had vanished.

The only one who could still see Paris was Riddick. He ran back to the sled when he heard the shotgun blast, and arrived in time to see a horde of predators fighting over the ravaged body. Within seconds they gutted him open like a fat white turkey and devoured him from the inside out.

Riddick saw a female flap down with a youngling on its back.

He watched in disbelief as the female, unable to find any scraps, whipped the youngling into its jaws, and began to chew it down. Other creatures turned on each other, caught up in a horrific feeding frenzy.

Then his night-vision eyes saw something even more ominous. A flock of predators were circling Audrey. The creatures hovered intently, as if the little girl exuded some powerful scent.

Fry saw nothing, but she could hear savage feeding sounds in the blackness. She turned and saw Riddick moving closer, gleaming eyes fixed on Audrey.

"What do you see, Riddick?"

"Hunger," he said quietly.

The train moved slowly across the thick darkness. *Like crossing a crocodile swamp*, Fry reflected, holding her light aloft. After what happened to Paris, she'd benched the umbrella torch in favor of an industrial flare. At least she'd have more warning when it started to burn out. She checked the remaining bottles. Down to four.

Johns and Imam were back in harness, their handlights beaming a path, while Audrey and Rashad walked side-guard, both carrying bottle torches.

Up ahead, Riddick's light bobbed like a distant buoy.

Audrey looked back at Fry. "We getting close?"

It was a good question. But only Riddick knew the answer. They'd all been blindly following the light on his back.

"Can we pick up the pace?" Fry called.

Sweating like a mule, Johns bristled at her prodding. "If you think you can do better . . ."

Imam's arm swatted his chest. Johns stopped and looked where Imam was pointing. A sled track waffled the ground in front of them. They'd been walking in circles.

Johns lifted his shotgun and flicked the laser sight. The red pencil beam found Riddick about ten yards ahead. He had stopped, and seemed to be waiting for them.

Riddick sensed the shotgun's laser on his back. He could always count on Johns to do the expected. He heard the others shuffling closer, but didn't turn around.

"Never could walk a straight line, huh?" Johns growled, behind him.

"Stay in the light, everyone!" Imam warned. "Rashad, everyone!"

Audrey came to Riddick's side. "What?" she whispered urgently. "What's going on?"

"Listen."

"We crossed our own tracks," Fry said accusingly.

"Why have we circled?" Imam put in. "Are we lost?"

"Oh, he ain't lost," Johns smirked knowingly. "But he'd love to lose a few of us and still get those cells back to—"

"*Listen.*"

An electric chittering crackled through the darkness, like static from a million speakers—or the scratching of a million claws. The sound swirled across the cold night wind in rising gusts.

"Canyon ahead," Riddick explained. "Circled to buy some time. Gotta think."

Imam looked at Fry. "I think we must go. Now!"

"Dunno if it's wise," Riddick drawled. "That your local Death Row up there . . . Especially with the girl bleedin'."

Scowling, Johns gave Fry a quick once-over. "What're you jaw-jackin' about? She ain't cut."

"Not her." Riddick donned his goggles and looked back at Audrey. "Her."

Seconds later it hit them like a club. The little girl was having her period.

"Oh God, honey," Fry muttered, "you should have told us if . . . Is he right? Are you bleeding?"

Audrey set her jaw defiantly. "You mighta left

me there alone . . . back at the ship. That's how come I didn't say anything . . ."

It's true, Fry thought, suddenly alarmed. The others exchanged worried glances.

"Aw, this can't be happening to me," Johns moaned.

Riddick ignored him. "They been nose-open for her ever since she left," he said softly. "They go off blood."

Imam put an arm around the little girl's shoulder. "We must keep her close, then. She'll be safe if we put her between—"

Riddick slowly shook his head. "There is no safe."

A howling chatter floated up from the canyon like a challenge.

13

The universe was collapsing on Fry.

She stood in a fragile bubble of light, listening to the mad symphony squealing in the canyon ahead. Above her, the blackness seethed with clickering death. Behind them the constant wail of wind-swept bones. And around her, the desperate sucking wheeze of their breathers swelled the monstrous cacophony squeezing in on her.

The terrible sounds, the leaden blackness, the pitiless horror devouring them one by one, crushed what remained of Fry's spirit.

"It's not gonna work," she rasped. "We gotta go back."

Johns pounced. His expression twisted into a triumphant smirk. "Hey, *you're* the one who got me out here, turned me into a goddamn sled dog. And now you expect me to go back like a *whipped* dog?"

"I was wrong," Fry said patiently. "I admit it.

My fault okay? *Now let's just go back to the ship.*"

"I dunno," Johns mused. "Nice breeze, wide open spaces—you know, I'm startin' to enjoy myself out here."

"Are you fucking high again? Just listen to . . ."

"No, no, you're right Fry. What's to be afraid of? My life is a steaming pile of meaningless toadshit anyhow. So I say mush on! Canyon's only a couple hundred meters—after that we're in skiff city!" Johns reminded, looking around at the others.

He turned back to Fry, jaw set in a nasty scowl. "So why don't you butch up, stuff a cork up that kid, and get . . ."

Imam moved beside Fry. "She's the captain. We should listen to . . ."

Johns looked at him in mock surprise. "Listen to her? Her? When she was willing to sacrifice us all?"

Suddenly the breathers went silent. Fry felt their eyes on her but she was too drained to defend herself.

"What's he talking about?" Audrey asked quietly.

Before Fry could answer, Johns stepped in. "During the crash she . . ."

"This does not help us, Johns," Fry said, voice rising over his.

". . . She tried to blow the whole fucking passenger cabin," Johns finished, staring at her. Daring her to deny it. "Tried to kill us . . ."

"Just shut the noise, okay?" she said lamely.

But the bully in Johns was enjoying himself.
". . . Tried to kill us in our sleep." He went on, eyes
gleaming in triumph. "Paris had it right . . . we are
disposable. We're just walkin' ghosts to her."

"Would you SHUT YOUR FUCKING BLOW
HOLE!"

Her voice came out a pained screech as she attacked, fingers clawing for his mocking eyes. Johns
shunted her aside with one hand, and lifted his
weapon with the other. He looked around.

"We're not alive because of her—we're alive *in
spite of her*."

Fry reeled at the edge of the light, burnt-out,
beat-up, and bent over with guilt.

"We cannot go through there," she insisted
hoarsely. For a moment she considered stepping
into the darkness and letting the predators decide.
Johns's smug voice pulled her back.

"How much you weigh right now, Fry? Huh?"
he brayed, lording it over her.

Disgusted, Imam stepped between them and
pushed him back. "Fine, fine, you've made your
point," the monk said calmly. "We can all be
scared."

Johns yanked a percussive flare and smacked the
butt against Imam's chest. Hard enough to ignite
the flare—and get the monk out of his face.

"Verdict's in," Johns yelled, lifting the flare like
a sword. "The light moves forward."

*   *   *

This train of fools is shrinking fast, Fry reflected wearily.

Rashad had slipped into harness next to Imam, while Fry manned rear-point. There were no more side-guards. Rashad had rigged an umbrella torch on the sled, but their circle of light had dimmed significantly.

Up ahead, Johns fell into step with Riddick. Disturbed by Johns's flare, Riddick pulled down his goggles.

"Ain't all of us gonna make it," Johns confided.

Riddick snorted. "Just realized that, huh?"

A flurry of clicking shadows blew past them. Johns blasted the darkness, driving the sounds away, and reminding everyone of who packed the firepower.

He turned back to Riddick. "Six of us left. If we could get through that canyon and lose just one, that'd be quite a fucking feat, huh? A good thing, right?"

"Not if I'm the one," Riddick snapped, annoyed by his ingratiating whine. He started walking away.

"What if you're one of five?"

Riddick paused. "I'm listening."

From a distance, Fry watched the two men talking. It was odd to see Johns and Riddick walking side by side, like equals. *More like partners*, Fry noted, suddenly suspicious.

Audrey noticed too. "What are they doing up there?" she muttered.

"Talking about the canyon, I suppose," Imam

assured her. "How to get us through . . ."

Riddick was listening to Johns's plan with rapt fascination. *Something my old cellmate Headhunter might of dreamt up*, he mused, eyes scanning the darkness ahead.

"Look it's hellified stuff," Johns said, voice low and sincere. ". . . But no different than those battlefield doctors when they have to decide who lives and who dies. It's called 'triage,' okay?"

"Kept calling it murder when I did it."

Johns smiled. "Either way, figure it's somethin' you can grab onto."

As they slowly marched toward the chattering canyon, Riddick calculated the options. *Think like a scumbag and the answer's easy*, he decided.

"Sacrifice play," Riddick muttered. "Hack up one body, leave it at the start of the canyon. Like a bucket of chum."

Johns gave him a triumphant grin. "*Travel* with it," he whispered proudly. "There's a cable on the sled. We can drag the body behind us."

Riddick had to admit Johns had thought it through. "Nice embellishment."

"Don't wanna feed these land sharks—just keep 'em off our scent," Johns explained, pleased with himself.

A hundred corpses wouldn't cover your stink, Riddick thought. But he was curious. He glanced back at the caravan. "So which one caught your eye?"

"Don't look, don't look, don't look . . ."

Johns's warning was more than paranoia. Behind them, Fry was watching them intently. *They're up to something*, she thought, instincts bristling. A vague sense of danger nibbled at her belly.

"Imam, slow down," she called in a hushed voice.

"What?" Confused, the monk paused to look at her.

"Don't stop, just slow down," Fry said, eyes still on the point men. "Little more space between us and them."

"I would rather we all stay . . ."

Fry turned and gave him a warning stare. "Just do as I say. Please."

Imam finally understood what she couldn't say. Brow furrowed with grave concern, he peered at the two men ahead.

"What's her name anyway?" Riddick knew, but he wanted Johns to say it.

"What do you care?"

Riddick shrugged and strode ahead. "I don't."

"Then let's not name the Thanksgiving turkey okay? I assume you still got a shiv?"

As it dawned, Riddick paused. "What—you expect me to do it?"

Johns seemed surprised by his reluctance. "What's one more to you? Like this is the one that sends you to hell?"

Comes to deep psycho, ol' Headhunter's an amateur, Riddick conceded. He shook his head admiringly. "Oh you're a piece of art, Johns. They ought to hang you in a museum somewhere." He turned and started walking to the canyon. ". . . Or maybe they should just hang you."

Johns hurried to catch up with Riddick. "All-right, *I'll* do the girl. You keep the others off my back." Actually he was looking forward to it. He owed Fry payback.

Riddick stopped, head cocked as if reconsidering.

"Aw, don't tell me you're growin' scruples," Johns prodded.

"Just wonderin' if we don't need a bigger piece of chum."

Johns angled his head at Imam. "Like who—the Sheik?"

Riddick smiled. *"Like Johns."*

As their eyes met, Johns lifted his weapon and fired.

The moment Fry heard the blast she knew it wasn't aimed at the predators. "Bring the light!" she shouted. She could still see Johns's flare but Riddick's handlight was gone.

Audrey came running to her side. "What're they doing? What're we . . . ?"

Without answering, Fry sprinted toward the streaking flare ahead.

Riddick was fast but the blast scorched his arm as he grabbed the shotgun and jerked it skyward. Something above them shrieked and loud feeding sounds erupted as the two men grappled for the weapon.

Johns's flare fell to the ground, creating an arena of illumination but each time they lurched into shadow, fast-clicking predators attacked—talons raking at the struggling men. Riddick and Johns wheeled, still wrestling for the shotgun, and gang-aimed at the squealing shapes. The blast drove them back—but not very far.

The creatures flapped wildly around the dim circle of light, like huge chittering vultures, waiting for a victim to fall. Riddick wrested the shotgun free, but Johns smacked it out of his hands. The weapon spun to the ground, but as Johns lunged, Riddick kicked it into the night. When Johns turned, he saw Riddick's shiv, wagging at him like a scolding finger.

"Gotta stay in the light, Johns, that's the only rule," Riddick said hoarsely.

Johns circled at the edge of the flare's light. Riddick feinted and jabbed, pushing Johns against the wall of darkness. Then Johns's foot stumbled over something. Desperately he scooped it up. A bone . . . a *club*.

"Bring whatcha got," Johns growled, suddenly confident. He was finally in his element, kill or be killed. He felt a rush of exhilaration as he hefted the heavy bone. "C'mon Trash-Baby, let's take the roof off."

Riddick found his own bone-club, whipped it against Johns's chest with a quick snap, then jumped out of range. Roaring, Johns swung hard. Bone-clubs clashing, they circled each other, grunting like cavemen. Riddick took his time, patience honed by a hundred prison fights and a decade of accumulated rage.

Johns swung again and missed. Costly error.

Riddick smacked Johns's club hand, breaking his fingers. Yowling, Johns dropped the weapon. An instant later he lunged, scrambling for the flare with his other hand. Suddenly he froze, eyes bulging in astonishment.

"Remember that moment?" Riddick whispered, voice hot against Johns's ear as he drove the shiv into his back. Riddick jerked the blade along Johns's spine, then jumped aside to avoid the oily red geyser of blood gushing from the wound. Blindly Johns crawled toward the flare's fading glow. Riddick dogged him every agonized step, talking him down to hell.

"Shoulda never took the chains off, Johns. You were one brave fuck before. Oh man, you was Cock Diesel with your gauge . . ." Trembling with primal fury Riddick ripped the badge from Johns's heaving chest. ". . . with that badge . . . with your chains. Oh yeah, you was Billy Bad-Ass . . ."

Without warning Johns dove for the fallen shotgun and snatched it with his good hand.

"*And I'm still Billy Bad-Ass!*" he rasped, sweeping the weapon around.

The red laser sight drilled into . . . blackness. Riddick had vanished.

Then he heard a rapid *clicking* behind him. Johns awkwardly grabbed the flare with his broken fingers and whirled in time to see a huge black shape looming closer. He fired, blasting the predator back but the flare dropped from his stiff, throbbing fingers. The hairs on his neck bristled and he spun around as a second creature rushed at him. Johns pulled the trigger.

Nothing happened. Screaming soundlessly as if trapped in a nightmare, Johns hurriedly ratcheted the weapon for another shot. The ejected shell fell beside the flare and in that instant Johns realized it was red.

He'd loaded a red morphine shell in the dark. It was the last rational thought he had before the beast's talons skewered his armpits like corn forks, and lifted him off the ground. The creature stared at him blankly, with deceptively gentle *clicking-cooing* sounds.

Gibbering and drooling with mindless terror Johns opened his mouth to scream. It never came. The predator reared back its horned head and slammed it forward. It rammed Johns with the full force of its skull-blade—splitting him in half like a lobster. As Johns's greasy organs splashed out in a steamy heap the creature began chewing his face off . . .

14

Fry, Imam, Audrey and Rashad rushed through the blackness as shotgun blasts bolted like lightning behind them. They were stumbling, running, trying to backtrack along the sled marks. Suddenly panicked that there wasn't enough light, Fry turned to see if she was being pursued—and crashed into something.

"Back to the ship, huh?" Riddick challenged. He'd been standing in the dark, waiting for them.

"Get out of our way," she said breathlessly.

Riddick stayed where he was, blocking their retreat along the sled track. "So everybody huddles together till the lights burn out? Until you can't see what's eatin' you? That the big plan?"

"Where's Mr. Johns?" Imam demanded.

"Which half?"

Imam's face went sickly pale in the dull light. "You mean . . ."

They all looked back where they'd last seen

Johns, faces reflecting remorse, disbelief, and raw terror. "Gonna lose everybody out here . . ." Audrey wailed, her eyes welling up.

"He died fast," Riddick snapped. "And if we got any choice, that's the way we should all go out." He turned to Audrey and bent close. "Don't you cry for Johns," he whispered gently. "Don't you dare."

Numbly she nodded. At that moment they both knew her life was in his hands. Riddick slowly started marching back to the canyon. Audrey fell into step behind him. After a few seconds Fry, Imam and Rashad reluctantly followed.

With Riddick leading and Imam and Rashad pulling the sled, they soon reached the entrance to the canyon. Ahead of them lay the gauntlet, and the blackness was in full cry. Without his goggles Riddick could see the horror waiting for them.

His jaguar eyes recognized the winged shapes perched everywhere like huge gargoyles on a ravaged cathedral. They loomed and hovered, thrashing about in constant movement, skull-blades clashing as they fought, fed and mated with savage ferocity. Their cries echoed hellishly in the canyon, rising above the snapping of bone and rending of flesh as they tore each other apart.

Some of the creatures slouched on the canyon rim, watching the approaching party with the pitiless intensity of falcons scanning a file of geese. The survivors pressed forward, weary faces reflecting their stark dread at what lay ahead.

Only Riddick seemed unafraid, but he'd written himself off years ago. For all intents and purposes he was dead—a walking corpse—about to be consumed like some unholy Eucharist, on behalf of a perverse God. *What difference does it make?* he thought grimly. *Either way I'm fodder for the eternal plan. Shit rolls downhill.*

"How many do you see?" Fry asked.

Riddick winked at Audrey and shrugged. "Only one or two."

They bought it.

"Audrey?" Fry said in her best military manner.

The little girl snapped to attention. "Three full bottles," she reported. "But almost time to refill."

Fry gave Riddick a rueful smile. "Doesn't seem like enough to turn back on—does it?"

He heard her. She was telling him it was his call. "Only see one way," he told them. "Turn the sled over, and drag it like that . . . Girl down low. Light up everything we got—and run like dogs on fire."

Imam nodded thoughtfully. "The sled as a shield . . . It might work." The drag sled's sharp steel sides were bent in a horseshoe shape. Without the power cells to support—and turned upside down—they made excellent runners. With Audrey crawling beneath, she had protection from an air attack. He gestured to Rashad and they went to work.

Fry wasn't convinced. "And what about the power cells?"

"I'll take those," Riddick said.

She calculated the possibilities. None were good.

Riddick had eliminated his captor. The witnesses couldn't be far behind. "We're just here to carry your light, aren't we?" Fry said, voice barbed with contempt. "Just the goddamn torch bearers."

Riddick didn't seem to hear. "Let's drop back," he called. "Boot up!"

As he walked away Fry noticed her torch flame was fading. She dropped down to one knee to refill the reservoir. With just the pilot light burning, Fry never saw the large shadow looming behind her.

Something made Riddick turn in time to see the creature stealing up on Fry. It spread its taloned wings as if waving goodbye. Riddick moved but he knew he'd never make it.

Abruptly Fry's torch flared, belching fire. The creature shrank back as Fry turned and walked toward him. *Doesn't know how close she came to being hamburger*, Riddick thought, turning back. *Ignorance sure is bliss.*

They regrouped in the bone yard at the mouth of the canyon. The constant wailing of wind blowing through the pitted bones played surreal counterpoint to their panting urgency as they worked. Riddick used the loading straps to rig a body harness for the power cells. He'd be carrying over two hundred pounds, but needed to move fast. The harness would balance the weight. Engrossed in his task he forgot where he was for a moment. Not wise.

When he stood up to admire his handiwork, Riddick came face-to-face with a predator.

Riddick knee-jerked back, pulling his shiv as he moved. Then he realized it was dead. *Long gone*, Riddick mused, inspecting the fossilized skull. The remnant was propped up by other bones, making it seem like a museum display. *Nasty-looking beast, live or dead*, he decided. The hammer head was crowned by a large bone blade like the one that clove Johns. Below it dangled a reptilian spine as if the blade was linked directly to the nervous system rather than the brain. *Pure killer instinct.*

Then Riddick noticed something even more interesting. Twin echo-location sensors positioned behind the eye sockets on each side of the skull. As he studied the echo sensors he suddenly understood.

"Blind spot . . ." he whispered.

If he stood directly in front of the creature— nose to nose—he couldn't be "seen" by its echo locators. *Nice theory*, he thought ruefully. *Hate to test it.*

"May I bless you?"

Riddick turned and saw Imam, peering at him from behind a handlight.

The monk gave him an apologetic smile. "I've already done the others," he explained. "It's really quite painless."

Riddick snorted. "It's pointless."

"Well even if you don't believe in God, it doesn't mean He won't be . . ."

Imam's voice trailed off when he saw Riddick's savagely gleaming eyes drilling into his.

"You think someone could spend half their life in a slam with a horse bit in their mouth and not believe?" Riddick asked, voice slicing like a razor. "You think he can start out in some liquor store trash bin with an umbilical around his neck and wind up a company enforcer—and not believe?"

Riddick's finger jabbed Imam's chest. "Got it all wrong. I absolutely believe in God. *And I absolutely hate the fucker.*"

"He will be with us nonetheless," the monk reminded gently.

Riddick slipped into his harness and latched it tight. "Give my blessing to the girl. She'll need a spare."

They saddled up reluctantly, torches maxed out, burning non-stop as they sucked down O_2 for the final race.

Imam and Fry took the sled chains, Audrey rolled beneath the sled shield between the runners, and Rashad took point, his handlight boring a trail through the blackness. Riddick pulled the goggles over his eyes, having no desire to see the unspeakable horrors waiting for them.

Only one path anyway, he thought grimly. *Straight down the belly of the beast.*

Riddick raised his hand. "As fast as you can!" he shouted.

Fry looked at the enormous leaden weight strapped to his back. "You sure you can keep . . . ?"

"As fast as you can," Riddick repeated. Then he dropped his hand and they began their death-run.

In the hellish glare of their white-hot torches, the small band of survivors raced for their lives, knowing there was no going back. Set at maximum burn, their torches would flame out in a short time. Pulled by Imam and Fry, the sled moved easily on its runners as Audrey speed-crawled beneath. Rashad sprinted ahead, thick legs pumping while Riddick struggled after them, his face already tortured with severe oxygen depletion—and the sheer agony of hauling 200 pounds of stubborn mule-cargo. But somehow he managed to keep pace with the ghostly caravan.

The wind stretched their torch flames like burning wings as they entered the canyon running. Immediately predators began launching themselves from the rim. First came the hatchlings, smaller, shriller and faster—who streamed right into their faces, veering aside at the last moment, repulsed by the light.

Next came the feral squeals of killing, feeding and squabbling that filled the darkness overhead. Thin blue liquid spattered down on the survivors as they trotted doggedly through the clickering, shrieking nightmare.

"Don't look up," Riddick yelled hoarsely.

More blue liquid showered down on them, trailing the unmistakable stench of blood. Fry felt something brush her hair.

"Do not look up!" Riddick warned.

Too late. Fry's brain reeled as she glimpsed the monstrous cloud writhing overhead. A ceiling of clicking predators encircled the cusp of light; diving, sliding, weaving, darting—slashing each other in their eagerness to sound out the human prey below.

It was like looking into a sky of angry snakes.

Fry stumbled, overcome by the enormity of the horror.

"Keep going, keep going, keep going, keep going!"

Riddick's cry whipped her on like the devil's coxswain. Spurred by terror, she dropped her head and moved faster. More blue blood drizzled down followed by oozing chunks of entrails as the creatures cannibalized each other even as they stalked their human prey. *Could this be hell?* Fry wondered dazedly. It didn't really matter.

Then she heard Imam's voice floating through the insanity. "So dark the clouds around my way— I cannot see," the monk chanted. "But through the darkness I believe Allah leadeth me. I gladly place my hand in His when all is dim . . . And closing my weary eyes, lean on Him . . ."

Just the fact that he was still able to pray bolstered Fry's sagging energy. And she needed anything she could hold on to. The blood frenzy overhead had reached a mad crescendo and *whole corpses* were crashing down around them with sickening wet sounds, victims of mass slaughter.

Fry and Imam were forced to slalom through

steaming piles of shredded flesh, like some gro-
tesque obstacle course. Up ahead Rashad veered
too close to a fallen creature and its head blade
sliced his leg . . . drawing blood. Silently, the pilgrim pushed forward.

Up ahead the canyon narrowed into a choke
point. Fry saw it first.

"Riddick?" She screamed. "RIDDICK?"

Blocking the choke point was a twitching mound
of flesh—dead predators, slimy with blood and entrails.

"What?" Audrey yelled, alerted by Fry's panic.
"What is it?"

"It's a fucking staircase!" Riddick roared. "Go
over it! GO OVER IT!"

A fetid stench enveloped them like some thick,
noxious fog. The stink of diseased, rotting corpses
pulled the air from Fry's lungs. Acid bile burned
her throat as she abandoned all hope and attacked
the blood-greased wall of gutted predators.

Seeing Fry push forward gave Rashad courage.
Twisted with nausea he moved to Imam's side. The
monk gave him a small smile. "Allah . . ." was all
he said, but it was enough to rally what was left of
Ali's energy.

"*Allah*!" The pilgrim cried, moving up to light
the way.

Picking their way over the slimy pile of death
was treacherous. Each bloody corpse was barbed
with sharp talons and razor-edged skull blades. The
stench, the squishing rot beneath their feet, and the

relentless clicking chaos overhead walled them inside a hideous cocoon. Reeling and stumbling, they fought for each step.

All except for Riddick. Pain, exhaustion, horror, foul odors from the bowels of despair were old acquaintances. Years in prison had taught him how to lift mind from body and fly free. His consciousness hovered above his straining body like a miner's lamp. He was pure animal survival in hell's own slaughterhouse.

The worst of it was reserved for Audrey. On all fours beneath the sled-shield, the little girl found herself face-to-entrails with gutted corpses. It was like crawling through a steaming blood-swamp of rotting slime laced with barbed wire. But the rhythm of Riddick's pounding footsteps behind her merged with her ragged heartbeat, urging her on. Ignoring her revulsion she slid her hands over the stinking corpses, and kept pace with the sled. Until her palm pressed down on a hatchling—*and it squirmed to life!*

Instinctively she recoiled to avoid the snapping teeth and flapping talons—and rolled through the runners. Suddenly she was exposed, tumbling down the mound of rotting flesh.

At the same instant a dozen rabid shapes dove for the struggling girl. Rashad glimpsed what was happening and swung his light around.

"Audrey!" Fry cried.

As Rashad moved to help, he slipped and lost

his handlight. The beam spun and stopped again on
Audrey like a game pointer.

The little girl blindly scrambled for Rashad's
light and slid under the sled-shield. At the same
time a predator kamikazied into the shield, its skull
blade piercing the metal and nearly skewering the
little girl beneath. Caught in torchlight, the creature
began to sizzle, howling as it tried to rip free of
the shield. Trapped, Audrey was battered by the
steel runners as the burning predator trashed wildly.

As Riddick neared, the creature tore free. Enraged with pain the predator spun and blindly
pounced.

Poised at light's edge Riddick caught the crea-
ture beneath its wing talons, blunting the attack.
The predator's head reared back, coiling to bisect
Riddick with its skull blade.

But Riddick had learned watching Johns die.
With switchblade speed he yanked his shiv and
swept across the creature's belly, spilling blood and
intestines. Shrieking the creature dropped and slid
away, trailing its own bowels.

Gasping for breath Riddick turned and saw
Imam and Fry gaping at him, pale faces reflecting
stunned disbelief. Riddick shrugged. "Didn't know
who he was fuckin' with."

Imam's mouth fell open. *They were one person
short!*

The monk's composure disintegrated like a fractured mirror. He slogged through the sea of oily

flesh, his head swiveling back and forth. "Rashad!" he screamed. "RASHAD!"

"Get the girl back under!" Riddick ordered. "Keep going!"

Calling frantically, the monk staggered in circles. "RASHAD!"

"KEEP GOING OR I WILL!" Riddick warned, shouldering the power cells.

Suddenly Rashad floated into the light like a bloodstained angel, his torn, ravaged body held aloft by unseen forces.

With shocked amazement Imam realized the shredded remnants of flesh still clung to life. Imam stretched out his arms, fingers reaching desperately. Eyes bulging with effort, Rashad feebly lifted a bloody hand.

Then he was gone, jerked out of the light . . . out of existence.

At the moment Imam's faith teetered. The monk took a deep breath. *Abandon Allah's trust and my pilgrims died for nothing*, he reflected. He turned and took his place in front of the sled.

Four little Indians, Fry noted grimly as they flailed on through the frenzied chaos. After they crested the festering flesh heap, the canyon widened like the portals to paradise. The constant screeching grew fainter, falling behind them in the hellish slaughter pit.

Their footing also became more secure as they passed fewer and fewer gutted corpses until the ground was clear. Fry and Imam exchanged relieved glances. Audrey managed a deep breath as the stench faded. For the first time they shared the faintest hope that the nightmare might end.

Except for Riddick. His etched features remained as impassive as marble beneath the black goggles as he marched through the darkness.

The torches began to spit and sputter as they ran out of fuel. With a sinking feeling, Audrey listened to a fresh hail of blood drumming on the metal shield.

Less light, more blood, fresh kill zone ahead, she thought, trying to steel herself against the renewed assault. It never came.

Instead the drumming spatters of blood grew louder.

Abruptly, one torch died. Fry frantically yanked the lever and somehow it flared up again.

Noticing the sudden lack of smell, Imam cupped his hand to catch some of the blood drizzling from above. Fry did the same. She peered closely at the liquid in her palm and realized it had no color.

"Oh no," Fry moaned as she recognized the new danger pouring down on them. "No, no, no . . ."

"Rain . . ." Imam said, voice hushed with disbelief.

15

Caught in the downpour, the caravan slogged to a stop. One torch went out and would not relight. Their protective halo was being extinguished by the driving rain.

It was the final irony, but only Riddick was laughing.

"So where the hell's God now, huh?" he rasped, turning to Imam.

Already wrestling with his faith, the Muslim shook his head.

"I'll tell you where!" Riddick cried, shaking his fist at the sky. "He's up there PISSING ON ME!"

Fry wasn't impressed. *This ain't about you!* she thought, with a surge of rage.

"Riddick?" she said tersely. "How close?"

His ugly grin melted into an impassive mask as he slowly lifted his goggles. For long moments he stared into the rain-swept darkness as if gazing into a black crystal.

Fry's nerves were too frayed for patience and her future was fading with the torchlight.

"Tell me the settlement is right there!" she cried, clenched fists weakly pounding his chest. "RID-DICK! *PLEASE!*"

It was like flailing at the Sphinx. Unmoved by her outburst, Riddick continued to scan ahead, liquid eyes revealing nothing. Finally he turned and shrugged.

"We can't make it," he told her, face as blank as stone.

Fry sagged and felt Imam's arm around her shoulder. Too stunned to speak, she swayed in the dying torchlight, as the terrible squeals behind them swelled louder.

Prodded by the horrific sound, Riddick took Audrey by the hand, pulling her to a cavelike crevice in the canyon wall. "Here!" he shouted, waving at Imam and Fry. "Hide here!"

Imam half-carried Fry to the crevice as the clickering hordes circled overhead, swooping closer to their prey.

"Inside, *inside*! Riddick hissed, pushing Imam after Fry. As they crawled into the narrow fissure, the second torch died behind them.

Now there was only one light left—the one on Riddick's back.

Numbly, Fry watched the light bobbing as Riddick muscled the sled-shield over to the crevice—and slid it over the opening.

All light gone, they crouched in the fissure, listening to the fiercely chattering sounds outside. Finally Audrey voiced the question they were all afraid to ask.

"Why is he still out there?"

Fry couldn't answer. *He might be protecting us*, she thought. *Or burying us.*

The mud made the footing difficult. *Especially dragging two hundred pounds of dead weight*, Riddick noted as he strained to reach the top of a steep rise. The rain had intensified, making it difficult to see. His eyes had been customized to see in the dark, not through water.

Like some futuristic Sisyphus, doomed to an eternity of pushing a boulder up a mountain, only to have it roll back to the bottom, Riddick hauled the power cells up the soggy, crumbling hill. Every few feet he slid on the rain-soaked mud, the heavy cells pulling him down like an anchor. Each time he managed to dig in and begin again, until he reached the crest.

Half-expecting to meet another obstacle he stood on the hill peering through the hard rain and saw it.

The Promised Land, Riddick exulted, looking down at the settlement. *From here it's all downhill.*

As he strode over the rise, the cells followed, slithering through the mud like a serpent's tail.

It didn't take long to reach the skiff. The predators followed every inch of he way, hovering just beyond the faint circle of light as Riddick boarded the dark craft.

The creatures began hammering the frail shell as he connected the power cells to the battery bay. Suddenly the interior lights blinked on.

As the ship came to life, the hammering stopped. There was only the drumming rain and the warm brightness inside. *Free at last*, Riddick exulted, slipping the goggles over his eyes.

He began a pre-flight integrity check. But as his fingers ran over the instruments, his mind kept going back to the people he'd left in the canyon. *Don't be sucked in*, he told himself. *Good intentions kill faster than bullets.*

Prison philosophy didn't help. A gnawing sense of urgency drew him to the hatch. He stood there, staring at the rain-drenched chaos beyond the skiff's cozy arc of light. Torn between survival and redemption.

He tried to blot out the images of the little girl being torn from her burrow like a field mouse and ripped open by relentless talons. Nothing worked. At last, like some hard-core addict losing his war against drugs, Riddick made certain he would never return to the canyon.

Very deliberately Riddick lifted the handlight, and smashed it against the hull. Then he stepped inside and shut the hatch behind him.

"He's not coming back, is he?"

Again Audrey voiced their deepest fear.

Crouched down in the bleak sanctuary Fry tried to figure it out. *If he wants us dead, why lead us here?* She looked at Imam, checking his face.

"Did Riddick say anything to you?"

Imam shook his head.

A shock of recognition bolted through Fry's brain. *She could see Imam's face.*

"There's light in here," she said in a hushed voice.

Imam looked up and spotted a soft glow above them. He stood and climbed the canyon wall. There were tiny blue-white lights clinging to the rocks like phosphorescent coral. Imam plucked a few. As he examined the glowing nodules they began to writhe in his palm. They were alive.

"What are they?" Fry asked, voice strained.

Imam came down and held out his hand. "Larva."

"Glow worms," Audrey corrected, eyes gleaming in the dim light.

Call it what you will, Imam thought. He knew it was a miracle. A sign from Allah that his prayers had been heard. His faith flooded back, reviving his parched spirit.

A spark of realization shot through Fry's brain. "How many bottles we got?" she asked, rummaging hurriedly. "Empty ones . . . as many as we can scrounge."

It was a good idea, but it took a long time. Even half-full of glow worms, the liquor bottle emitted a weak illumination, barely enough to ward off the predators.

"More, more," Audrey said in a whispered chant, "we need more."

The pile of worms climbed higher. Inch by inch the phosphorescent larvae brightened their cramped world. Finally they managed to fill two bottles. *One to travel with*, Fry thought. She rigged a secure harness for the bottle and strung it around her neck.

Imam understood. So did Audrey, but she didn't like it. She started to beg Fry to stay, then stopped, knowing it was useless.

Fry patted the little girl's shoulder and moved to the entrance. Cautiously, Fry pushed aside the sled-shield and extended the bottle. Immediately the relentless *clicking* receded. Without looking back, Fry slipped outside.

The rain drummed down, making it difficult to see more than a few feet ahead. *Which was just as well*, Fry decided, aware of the clicking predators swooping around her protective bubble of light.

Beyond hope, Fry's anger maintained her will as she pushed up the dark rise. The sled tracks were long gone, washed out by the deluge. The only direction she could follow was up.

After what seemed hours of sliding and clawing through the mud, Fry stood on the crest. Drenched and exhausted, her breath coming in rapid gasps, she saw a distant light. She made out the outline of the settlement and knew the light came from the skiff.

Jolted by a sudden rage, Fry began to jog recklessly down the hill.

Back in the narrow cave, Imam and Audrey huddled together, bent over the bottle of glow worms. Imam murmured his prayers as the little girl dozed fitfully, dreams and reality appearing in violent fragments. She was awakened by a rapid knocking on the shield.

At first she thought it was Fry, knocking to get back in. But the scrabble of clicking squeals pressing around the entrance bolted through her belly like electricity. Paralyzed with terror, Audrey watched Imam crawl to the shield to make sure it was wedged shut.

She saw Imam put his face to a slit in the shield and peer out into the darkness. Audrey shouted a warning—but as she opened her mouth the shield cracked open.

A talon pierced the shield a few inches from Imam's head. As he jerked back a second crashed through the shield. He snatched the glowing bottle and brandished the light at the frantic flurry of blades, sawing at the edges of the shield.

In horrified fascination Audrey saw two blades actually sizzle and burn as the light came near. Screeching, the predators recoiled.

Imam placed the illuminated bottle closer to the shield, so the light could fill the gaps left by the predator's blades. Then he began to pray. But as he placed a protective arm around Audrey, she felt abandoned by God . . .

*   *   *

Riddick fiddled with the flight controls before rolling the skiff to the runway. For some reason he took his time, unable to strap himself in and take off. He kept peering out through the rain-soaked darkness, as if expecting someone.

He sat in the flight chair and checked the computer for the fourth time. All systems were primed for go. *Get in the wind, asshole*, Riddick urged, but he hesitated.

What if they make it over the hill?

So what? came his answer. *First come, first saved.*

But for the first time in decades a strange emotion gnawed at his certainty.

Every time you get noble, you get royally fucked, Riddick reminded himself. Still, he couldn't pull the flight trigger.

His instincts suddenly bristled. He stood up and opened the hatch. Pulling off his goggles Riddick peered through the darkness.

A dull light was bobbing towards the skiff, pursued by a dozen shadowy predators, talon-tipped wings ready to pounce.

Without hesitation Riddick dimmed the interior lights and activated he skiff's head beams. He pulled down his goggles as the figure ran into the bright light and stopped.

Startled, he realized it was Fry. And she didn't look happy to see him. She crouched in the head beams like a drenched cheetah ready to spring for his throat.

Riddick stepped outside, on the stairway. Below, Fry remained where she was, in the rain-fogged light beam. "Strong survival instinct," Riddick drawled. "Admire that in a woman."

Fry wasn't amused. "You're not leaving," she shouted. "Not until we go back for the others."

Riddick snorted, and turned away.

"I promised them we'd go back with more light," she called, moving to the stairs. "And that's exactly what we are going to do!"

Riddick paused and looked back at her. "Think you've mistaken me for somebody that gives a fuck!"

"What, you're afraid?" Fry jeered. She stood swaying in the rain as if daring him to attack her.

"Confusin' me with Johns now," Riddick corrected with a sly smile. "Fear was *his* monkey. I only deal in life and death. All that stuff in between? Some shade of gray my eyes don't see."

"I trusted you, Riddick!" Fry pointed at him, voice barbed with contempt. "Goddamn, I trusted that some part of you wanted to rejoin the human race."

His face remained impassive, mouth tight beneath the dark goggles. "Truthfully?" he said quietly. "I wouldn't know how."

Fry's hands dropped to her sides. She realized Riddick didn't play by anybody's rules. But she knew he had compassion. She had seen it out there.

He could have left them stranded. But he led them to safety before he made his run.

"Then wait for me," she yelled, voice ragged with desperation. "I'll go back myself. Just give me more light for them."

That got to him. Face taut, he tossed her the broken light.

Fry threw the light aside. "Just come with me!" she cried, sensing he was wavering.

He resisted the impulse. "Got a better idea. Come with *me* . . ."

Fry looked at him as if repelled. But Riddick knew she was considering it.

"You're fuckin' with me," she said finally. "I know you are."

"Course I am," he admitted. "But that doesn't mean I won't leave you here. If you believe *anything* about me, better be *that*."

For a long moment the only sound was the driving rain. Fry's mind was racing backward . . . to Owens screaming, to that moment she pushed the PURGE button . . . fifty lives to save her own sweet ass, to every steep, treacherous step it took to get her off the trash colony where she was hatched . . . to here.

"No, you see I *promised* them," Fry said, stepping back, one foot in shadow. "I have to . . . I have to go and . . ." She paused, rain streaking down her stricken features.

It was clear she was bleeding resolve. Riddick could see it. He could smell it like the predators waiting for her to step back too far. So he kept slashing away at her will.

"Step aboard, Carolyn," he said calmly.

"I can't . . . I can't . . ."

Riddick stepped out into the rain and extended his hand. "Here," he whispered hoarsely. "Make it easy on you."

Her eyes locked on his, unblinking in the windswept storm. "Don't do this to me . . ."

"Just give me your hand," he said, leaning down the stairway. His streaked goggles were skull-dark sockets above his grim mouth.

Fry started to lift her hand, then dropped it. "But they . . . they could still be . . ."

"No one's gonna blame you," he said, in a calm soothing voice, like a priest hearing confession. "C'mon. Take my hand and save yourself, Carolyn."

Hearing him speak her name convinced Fry. Hesitantly, she lifted her hand and felt his fingers close strong and secure around hers.

With sudden fury Fry yanked—dragging him down the gangway.

Both of them sprawled in the rain-spattered mud, the hovering creatures screeching in anticipation. Fry rolled and wedged a knee against his throat, hard.

"Listen, you asshole, I *am* the captain of this ship—and I will not give up on them!" She shouted, gasping for breath. "I will not leave *any-*

one on this rock with those things—even if it means . . ."

In a snake-swift blur Riddick's neck was free and his shiv digging into her throat like a venomous fang. Too exhausted for fear Fry waited for him to slice her jugular and toss her to the predators.

But when their eyes met, his expression was strangely calm. He regarded her with bemused curiosity, his blade gently stroking her neck.

"You would die for them?"

The question hung in the drumming rain.

"I would try for them," Fry said finally.

Riddick snorted and looked away. "You hardly know them."

Fry pounded his shoulder angrily and struggled to her feet. "I'm sorry . . . I'm sorry but I *do* feel fear—*theirs, too*!" She ranted, eyes half-closed against the rain. She bent down and glared at him. "Godammit, Riddick . . . Yes! I would die for them."

He didn't answer, face as blank as his rain-streaked goggles.

16

I must be totally insane, Fry thought as she slogged through the downpour, aware of the clicking predators swarming around the sickly pale illumination of the glow worms. *Back in hell's toilet by choice.*

Goggles off, Riddick marched ahead, leading her back to the canyon. Time and again he would recoil as a predator zoomed past the edge of the light. And every weary step through the storm-drenched darkness was dogged by the relentless clicking.

Once back inside the canyon Fry realized that it would be difficult locating the cave sanctuary amid the hundreds of unfamiliar shadows. Numbly, she trailed Riddick, feeling foolish, as if returning for Audrey and Imam had been a neurotic impulse.

Riddick didn't seem to think so. Ever since leaving the skiff he'd been focused. *One last pass and I'm clean*, he told himself, moving steadily through

the rain. Then he paused. His night-vision eyes
picked up a flurried knot of predators.

Runoff from the deluge had formed a huge pool
at the bottom of the hill, and the winged creatures
were gathered to drink. Riddick detoured around
them and scanned the canyon wall for familiar
landmarks.

All he found was flat black rock. But as he
moved along the wall, more predators floated down
to the watering hole.

A hard scrabbling sound awakened Audrey from
her nightmare.

The blades, she thought, pushing back against
the wall. She saw Imam crouched near the shield,
his spectacles glinting in the bottle's dim illumination.

Imam lifted his sword as the shield, rattled—
then moved . . .

As the shield fell aside, Imam rose up to meet
the attack. He stopped, blade poised in midair.

Fry stepped inside, followed by Riddick.

Audrey stared wide-eyed as if St. Nicholas had
just appeared from the fireplace with a sack of presents. "You came for us . . ." she said in disbelief.

Riddick scooped up the second bottle of glow
worms. "Yeah, yeah . . . we're all fuckin' amazed.
Anyone not ready for this?"

Imam managed a smile. Again his prayers had
been answered.

However, as they emerged from their sanctuary

he wondered how many prayers he had left. Driven by the wind, the rain was slanting down in sheets, and the darkness seethed with predators circling their meager light.

"Tighter, tighter," Riddick urged, leading the way. His eyes gleamed like black diamonds, searching for the rise. Then he saw it.

"Stop."

Audrey and Fry piled up awkwardly behind Riddick. Imam held the glowing bottle aloft and they stood silent, listening. There was nothing but the steady rainfall.

"I don't hear—"

Riddick clapped a hand over Fry's mouth. His enhanced vision could see the rise ahead. And a predator stood directly in front of them. The creature's hammerhead was bent, drinking the water pooled at the base of the muddy rise.

"Doesn't see us," Riddick's voice was warm against Fry's ear. "Wait for it to leave."

First error. The creature wasn't leaving. As they waited in the chattering downpour, other predators swooped down to drink at the widening pool. One by one they landed, until the pool became a major gathering place for the winged beasts.

Like blood-glutted gargoyles, fresh from their kills, Riddick thought, looking for a detour. There was none. The survivors behind him started to waver as the dreaded *clicking* sounds filled the darkness.

"Stay behind me!"

As Riddick spoke the predators shifted places in the pool and a narrow gap appeared. Without hesitation he decided. "Get behind me!" he hissed. "When I go, we go! Full throttle!" He took Fry's wrist, made sure everyone joined hands, and crouched down, waiting.

The creatures shoved for position as newcomers dropped in their midst.

"Ready, ready . . ." he chanted hoarsely, watching the winged shapes like a surfer studying monstrous waves. He glimpsed a brief parting in the sea of fangs and talons—and went for it.

Good timing. As Riddick dove forward, a pair of creatures broke into a furious squabble. Their wildly flapping wings widened the gap as other predators scuttled out of the way. Just as they reached the pool, the gap became a narrow passage.

Riddick ran headlong into the passage, half-dragging the others, all linked like paper dolls in a howling death-storm. Some of the creatures turned to "stare" blindly at the screaming intruders, their echo beams sensing one long shape.

Legs spraying water, Riddick and the others crashed through, scattering the predators long enough to reach the rise. There, they scrambled desperately over the rain-slicked mud, feet churning to outrun the creatures clawing after them.

Audrey lost her grip and began back-sliding toward the pool. Riddick snatched her by the ankle and yanked her back as a claw lashed out.

In the same motion Riddick muscled the little girl up the rise and heaved her bodily over the crest. Audrey tumbled and slid down the other side.

Only problem was, Audrey had the light.

"You know the way?" Riddick shouted, but Fry and Imam rushed past and disappeared over the crest. Riddick paused to catch his breath and glanced back. Second error.

They were coming in force, spreading over the rise like a writhing black shroud.

Riddick ran, galloping over the crest, and recklessly bounding down the muddy hill to catch up with Imam, Fry, and Audrey. Their glowing bottles bounced wildly in the darkness ahead, as Riddick scrambled to elude the talons raking at his heels.

Fry, Imam, and Audrey headed for the building outlined in the distance. Breathing in tortured gasps they spilled around a corner and saw . . . the lights of the skiff.

Racing behind them, Riddick saw the trio vanish around the corner leaving him . . . in total darkness. At the same time a winged shape floated down directly in front of him.

Riddick froze in his tracks. The creature had its back to him, but it sensed something. Slowly, the predator turned, its blade-crowned skull six inches away from Riddick's shimmering eyes.

In that instant Riddick made an extreme choice. He stepped close enough to the rapidly clicking creature to smell its rotten breath—and stand in its blind spot.

The razor-tipped skull twitched from side to side in confusion, scenting human prey but unable to locate him with its sensors. Riddick swayed in a snake charmer's dance, staying nose-to-nose with the creature—keeping himself in the blind spot.

The stench frayed at his nerves and Riddick felt a flicker of uncertainty. To his shuddering relief the creature turned away. But the uncertainty lingered.

A spidery prickle crawled up his neck. Even before he heard the rapid *clicking*, Riddick knew. Another predator had landed behind him.

As ruthlessly efficient as the demon beasts stalking him, he slashed and spun. The move gutted one predator and the others immediately began snatching bites and chunks of their wounded kin. Without warning it all collapsed on Riddick as he realized that he had an essential part in the gruesome ballet swirling around him. Like the cosmic snake eating its eternal tail, he created and destroyed his own reality.

Perhaps he glimpsed God's own mirror.

Whatever happened, it blew his soul.

Exhausted and breathless, Imam and Audrey staggered aboard the skiff.

Below them, in the light of the head beams, Fry stood gasping for air, waiting. For Riddick.

Long seconds went by, then minutes, as her eyes swept the dark rain.

"Captain . . ." Imam called out. He wanted her to board the skiff, but knew why she couldn't. A pang of shame tempered his fear, and he prayed for forgiveness.

Face streaming-wet and hair drenched flat in the wind-driven deluge, Fry stared at the blackness beyond the light. She listened hard but the monotonous drumming of rain washed away the sounds.

Then she heard it. A ragged howl floated over the wind. Without hesitation Fry jumped aboard the skiff, snatched the glow-worm bottle from Audrey's neck and dashed outside. Feet sliding in mud she plunged through the darkness, guiding by the rising screams.

A shrieking blade flashed past her face. Fry ducked and spotted her attacker.

Riddick. Face spattered blue with predator's blood, writhing body caked with mud, he knelt beside a freshly gutted kill—his blade slashing wildly at the creatures gathered at the edges of the light.

"It's me, it's me, *IT'S ME*!" Fry shouted. As she secured the bottle around his neck, Fry saw his face clearly in the glow. Riddick had changed. His stony-white features and liquid, black eyes reflected a very human emotion. *Naked terror.*

Fry grabbed his armpits and lifted, but her feet couldn't find purchase in the mud.

"C'mon, Riddick," she rasped in his ear. "I said I'd die for *them*—not you!"

He managed to get his feet under him and with

her help, started walking back to the skiff. Behind them predators dove down to feed on Riddick's kill in the sudden dark.

A wave of *clicking* sounds followed Riddick and Fry's stumbling footsteps toward the skiff's beacon lights. Fry hadn't checked Riddick for open wounds so she rotated him as they plowed through the rain—both spinning like dancers in a macabre waltz—hoping to throw the predators off his blood scent.

"Just ten steps," she muttered, urging him on past the swooping predators. "Keep turning, *keep turning* . . . that's right . . . others're already 'board waitin' for us right now . . . five steps, *c'mon*, almost there, Riddick . . . almost there . . . we're *almost . . .*"

A hard jolt staggered them both. Suddenly the *clicking* stopped.

In the drumming silence, Fry and Riddick found each other's eyes. They knew what had happened. Someone had been slashed from behind—and was bleeding . . .

But who?

Riddick slowly shook his head. "Not for me . . ."

Fry gave him a surprised look. Then vanished. Torn from his arms by a ghastly black cyclone of ravenous fury.

No scream, Riddick thought numbly.

No cry. No final words. Nothing but the rain— and a pitch-black universe.

This is the way the world ends . . . not with a bang but a whimper, Riddick recited prayerlike as he dragged himself through the downpour toward the skiff.

17

The fabric wings ignited when the skiff reached escape velocity. For a long moment it hung like a burning moth against the immense blackness. Until the wings disintegrated and it disappeared into space.

After a few hours, distant stars blinked into view, like city lights at the edge of a trackless desert. Riddick remained hunched over the control board, toggling through nav-charts with a bloody hand. *Just as easy coulda been me*, he told himself. But he knew better. Fry had come back for him.

At the rear of the skiff, Imam rolled out a prayer mat and knelt. He smiled at Audrey who was watching him curiously. "With so much prayer to make up for . . . just where I should . . . ?"

"I know where *I'd* start," Audrey snapped, curiosity spilling into contempt.

"Of course," Imam said apologetically. He

bowed his head. "Forgive me. Captain Fry gave her life . . ."

"She really died for us?"

The little girl's question drifted in the sudden silence. Up at the control board Riddick waited for the answer.

"Only Allah knows whether it was for us or herself," Imam said quietly. "Or even both." He lowered his head and began to pray.

Restless, Audrey joined Riddick at the control board. "Guess it's okay for us to talk now," she said hopefully.

Riddick didn't answer, his attention on the navcharts.

"So you can find us a shipping lane, right?" the little girl prattled on. "And then someone picks us up so we can go wherever we want? Maybe someplace . . . bright. With *showers*. Someplace like . . . well, sort of like where I came from, really."

When he didn't respond she went on. "You see, I was just running away when this whole thing started."

Riddick knew what she was getting at. She was a child alone in a vast, predatory cosmos. And she needed a guide.

"Only one problem with that plan," he said, goggled eyes still fixed on the board.

"What?"

Riddick plotted a course and a glittering swirl of stars swept across the windscreen. "Lotta questions,

whoever we run into. Might even be a merc ship,"
he explained, looking at her intently. "And I can't
have you . . . tellin' them . . . that I'm a con on the
outs. Now, can I?"

Something about his expression alarmed her.
Imam, too, glanced up from his prayer, alerted by
his strange tone.

"You see," Riddick chuckled, "*I was just running away when this whole thing started . . .*"

He was the only one amused. Suddenly afraid,
Audrey edged away from the board. "I wouldn't do
that, I swear. I won't tell them nothin' you don't
want me to."

Audrey's panic sparked Imam's instincts. Heart
racing, he stretched out his hand, fumbling about
for his blade.

"Swear to shit I wouldn't!" Audrey repeated,
voice shrill. "*I swear!*"

In the corner of his eye Imam spotted a glint of
steel and reached for it.

"Think our dyin' ain't quite done," Riddick said
thoughtfully.

The six words rattled like a snake in Imam's
brain. He unsheathed his blade and crouched on the
prayer mat. Audrey, too, seemed coiled to fight as
Riddick drew something from his belt.

It was metallic, with sharp edges. Johns's holobadge.

Carefully, he pinned the badge on his vest.

"Riddick's dead," he declared solemnly. "Call
me Johns."

Audrey gave Imam a small smile of relief. It would take her a while to understand Uncle Johns's sense of humor. But they still had light-years to cross.

Imam exhaled slowly. He put aside his weapon and murmured a prayer for all the lost pilgrims—especially Riddick . . .

Frank Lauria was born in Brooklyn, New York, and graduated from Manhattan College. He has traveled extensively and published sixteen novels, including five bestsellers and the novelizations of *Dark City, End of Days, Mask of Zorro,* and *Alaska*. He has written articles and reviews for various magazines and is a published poet and songwriter. Mr. Lauria currently resides in San Francisco where he teaches creative writing. A film project based on his Doctor Orient series is in development.